THE DEAR ONES

BERTA DÁVILA
THE DEAR ONES

Translated from Galician
by Jacob Rogers

3TimesRebel

First published by 3TimesRebel Press in 2023, our second year of existence.

Title: *The Dear Ones* by Berta Dávila

Original title: *Os seres queridos*
Copyright © Berta Dávila, 2022
Published with special arrangements with The Ella Sher
Literary Agency

Originally published by Edicións Xerais de Galicia, S.A.

Translation from Galician: Copyright © Jacob Rogers, 2023

Design and layout: Enric Jardí

Illustrations: Anna Pont Armengol

Editing and proof reading: Greg Mulhern, Carme Bou, Bibiana Mas

Maria-Mercè Marçal's poem *Deriva*:
© heiresses of Maria-Mercè Marçal

Translation of Maria-Mercè Marçal's poem *Deriva*:
© Dr Sam Abrams

Author photograph: © Adela Dávila

The translation of this book is supported by Acción Cultural
Española, AC/E

AC/E
ACCIÓN CULTURAL
ESPAÑOLA

Printed and bound by TJ Books, Padstow, Cornwall, England
Paperback ISBN: 978-1-7398236-8-9
eBook ISBN: 9781-7393236-9-6 / 978-1-7391287-4-6

www.3timesrebel.com

For Juanma; he knows why

PREAMBLE
TRIMEROUS
FLOWERS

TEN DAYS BEFORE CHRISTMAS, MY FRIEND LUCÍA SAID TO ME that a book that discusses its own writing is like a stillborn child, that it breaks the spell, that it strikes her not as literature but as something else, and that she finds that something boring. We're sitting on the plastic benches in an airport when she says this, waiting for them to announce the gate for her flight back to Madrid. I say I'm not sure that's true, and that if it is, I'm not sure it bothers me. She shrugs.

Lucía is going back home to spend some time with her family before she gets married at the end of December. I've driven her to the airport, wheeled suitcase and apathy in tow, to make the trip easier. I try to explain that when I write about writing, I'm not actually writing about writing, and that I would write about stockings and corsets if I worked in a lingerie store, or chlorine and cubic litres of water if I spent my time cleaning the bottoms of pools. I also try to explain that when I write about writing, writing belongs not to the world of ideas but to the world of objects, so that when I say a novel in a novel, or poem in a poem, I'm invoking them the way we might say *tree*, *house*, or *river*, not *deforestation*, *habitable*, or *hydrography*. She changes the subject and asks about my son and the novel I'm working on, which are the two subjects my friends always ask me about. Then she glances at the clock and at the runway on the other side of the glass and goes silent for a little while.

Planes are interchangeable places. Aside from being vehicles we use to travel to one place or from another, they're spaces outside of time, or where time takes on spatial dimensions. It doesn't matter what landscape unfurls beneath you when you're flying, it's how long you're in the air that counts. In an airport, what counts is how long you spend waiting. And while I wait with Lucía, I keep trying to explain that I started the book with the sincere intention of not talking about writing, because it was a novel about a mother and son, and if I was going to write about a mother and son without feeling caught in the middle, I needed the protagonist to be nothing like me.

In reality, I'm not sure it was a novel about a mother and son. I think it was a novel about certain kinds of bonds, and about the three stages of human life. I'd given it what felt like an evocative title: *Trimerous Flowers*. I whisper this to Lucía as if it's a secret of the highest order, but she has this unbearable habit where nothing animates her, as if she's incapable of expressing a trivial opinion, not even out of courtesy, and has to fully digest your every utterance before she can formulate her thoughts. So, when I tell her the title I picked out, she shrugs again and mutters something, a bit disoriented, because she hasn't had the time to conscientiously evaluate whether she likes it or not, the way she usually would, and I get the sense that she must be more apathetic about returning to Madrid than I'd thought.

The book was about a mother who loses her son in a traffic accident. She was a radio show host for a local station and lived alone. A few months after the accident, still grieving, she moved in with her grandmother, an elderly woman who had some sort of dementia and wasn't very mobile but was the only family the mother had left. Lucía asks if the grandmother resembles my grandmother María. I say probably, I'm sure she does, and detail some of my grandmother's behaviours over the past few months. For example, she almost always recognises me the moment I come into the room, but often forgets recent news or what year it is; she asks me about grades and exams, as if I'm still an undergraduate, or about the father of my son, as if Miguel and I had never split up. There are times when I can't help but feel that these are selfish mistakes, because she tends to forget the bits that she disapproves of, and asks to hear about a life that's not mine but sounds suspiciously similar to the life I suspect she envisioned for me. But I have no proof for this theory: my grandmother María also talks about long-dead friends as if they were still alive and visited her last week, forgets names and recipes, and mistakes the seasons of the year.

I had transferred my grandmother's various confusions to the grandmother in my book, although heightened, so that the character lived completely out of joint. The grandmother character's dementia was convenient for the mother character, because it meant she could be with another person without having to talk about her dead son. And the dementia of the grandmother's character meshed with the mother's grief: they were both somewhat detached from the world and of the frivolity of daily routine, and created their own instead, as if they found it strange to be alive but had no other alternative. The mother tended to her grandmother, and the two of them tended to a garden in spring. I wanted for them to plant tulips because they hold a special meaning for me and are the basis for the title, but I learned—to my frustration—that tulips have to be planted in winter. This had forced me to shift the timeline of the novel backwards by a few months and rewrite everything that happened in the winter so that it would happen in the autumn, and everything that happened in the autumn, in the summer. All so that the two of them could plant tulips in December, when you're supposed to. That was the first sign, albeit subtle, that the book didn't work. As trivial as it may sound, the entire project began to unravel after that discovery, and by the time I was explaining the plot to Lucía, I'd already become more or less convinced that there was something in the novel that would keep me from ever getting it right.

For the longest time, I've found airports unpleasant. I hate their constant temperature, that coolness typical of a pharmacy, with hardly any variation between different areas. And I hate their pretence of sterility. They might seem clean if not for small, localised disasters like an overflowing bin or a plastic tray with coffee all over it, abandoned by a traveller who'd spilled their drink and given up on trying to daub the catastrophe away with napkins. If you overlook those spots, airports seem perfectly clean, when in fact they're riddled with germs: a result of the constant movement of people on their way from one place to another.

Lucía says it must be hard to talk about mothers in a book. 'But I guess you have lots to say about it,' she then adds. I'm tempted to reply something to the effect that I've written about mothers and sons before, but I know that's not true. Whenever I've written about mothers and sons in the past, I've tried to do it stealthily, avoiding the trap. Over time, it turned into an uncomfortable proposition, a desire that sometimes took on the character of a duty: I was a mother, so I should, in some way, have been a mother in my fiction, too.

I always keep the mother and son in my books curled up in a still environment, trapped between two retaining walls that prevent them from expanding. They appear in minor anecdotes, self-enclosed and almost always inopportune, like a stain. These bubbles have the same effect on my stories as a dream, a ghost, a shadow, or a stray flower in the middle of a path. Sometimes I use them to foreshadow fears and ideas about the protagonist, and at others, they're a way for me to spill a drop of oil or coffee onto my otherwise immaculate page, bleeding through to the other side, like an aberration.

In public, I tend to say that I'm not capable of writing at length about mothers or sons because it's painful or difficult, but that's not the real reason. I knew that there was a book in it, and I knew why I'd been avoiding it for so long.

To begin with, I hated the vocabulary. The word *pregnancy*, for example. Or *baby*. I couldn't stand the word *embryo*, either, and I felt that the technical concepts we only have one word for always spoilt the poetry. The word *abortion*, of course. I've written about *abortion* and *embryos* without ever using the words abortion or embryo. Behind that omission was a sense of shame and fear, and a desire to keep these terms out of my writing, as if there were some words that didn't belong in literature and it was my job to keep them out. I found ways to talk about these things without using the commonplace words for them and, I admit, I was often proud of myself for it.

A few months ago, in an interview, a journalist I got along well with asked me what I thought about the growing popularity of Turkish soap operas. I replied that the themes in Turkish soap operas aren't all that distinct from the themes in Shakespeare's tragedies. The thought rang true to me, even if it was only a half-truth. Turkish soap operas, unlike Shakespeare's tragedies, are tasteless, or so I thought, although I couldn't have explained why, or why I thought that way. I ask Lucía if she thinks childbirth is a tasteless topic to write about. She says not particularly and talks about the transcendent moment when a person gives birth. 'Bringing a child into the light must be a moving experience,' she says. Apparently she finds it moving *to bring a child into the light*, as our saying goes, but it's not clear to me whether she feels the same about giving birth.

I tell Lucía that I was delivered by an emergency C-section, that they made a long, vertical incision down my mother's stomach, starting below her belly button, and that her scar hasn't faded and has actually grown over the years, turning into a sort of a thick, pinkish rope that runs down her lower abdomen. 'Now that would be tasteless to put in a book,' she says, though she doesn't clarify this point either. 'I don't know, it's hard not to think of stitches as tasteless, as too trivial,' she says after a moment. I defend myself by reminding her that I write about trivial things, and she replies that that may be true, but when I write about trivial things, I always stylise them. Maybe there are some wounds that are impossible to stylise, even for literature.

This brings me back to when Carlos came home from the grocery store last Tuesday. Since we moved in together, Carlos has taken care of most of the household chores. He knows when we need more milk or coffee, and how much fruit to buy so we don't run out of oranges and none of it rots in the bowl. I cook, do the dishes, and make the beds. He does the laundry and folds the clothes. We've never discussed this; it's a tacit distribution. He's able to keep track of the things that require some foresight, and I take care of the immediate tasks. That day, Carlos came back with apples and bananas. I was writing in the kitchen when he walked in, extremely distracted, and I looked right through him. He said, 'Sometimes I think you stare at me just so you can write about me later.' Then, 'Maybe you could write about this, except that you'd never say I bought apples and bananas, you'd say it was redcurrants and peaches, or something even worse.' This is how I stylise the trivial in literature: redcurrants and peaches in place of apples and bananas; bringing into the light instead of giving birth.

Some information about Lucía's flight finally appears on the departures screen; it's delayed, they'll announce the boarding gate in fifteen minutes. Before we say our goodbyes, she offers to buy me an orange juice at one of those airport bars where the signage is both too warm and too modern. Lucía doesn't drink coffee. I have to pick up my son from his music lesson in the mid-afternoon, but I still have plenty of time, and I accept her offer because I'm thirsty but also because Lucía is a great conversationalist and I owe her a goodbye. We've known each other for a long time. In fact, it was Lucía who introduced me to Miguel at a New Year's party I'd only gone to because, once again, I owed her a goodbye. I talk about how ATM screens and water fountain buttons are the dirtiest places in an airport, in that order. Nothing in the world could convince me to use an airport water fountain to quench my thirst.

I drink my juice and make idle chatter, asking about Lucía's plans with her family over the holidays and about all the details of her wedding. She takes a band of flowers out of a little box in her purse and shows it to me: she's thinking of wearing it around her head for the celebration. It's tacky, but I tell her that I love the idea and can't wait for the wedding, that I can't believe it's so soon. As she puts the band away, I see a tiny hortensia petal detach and fall off; I'm sure it used to be blue, and only turned pale and brown in the drying process. She tells me they're going to have their honeymoon in Lanzarote, the same place her parents honeymooned forty years ago. Lucía's enthusiasm about all these preparations puts me at a distance from her, but I don't think she notices that while she's talking, I'm busy throwing my book about the mother and son out of the window, convinced I've found yet another reason it doesn't work. There's a powerful truth in the words that have always stood out to me as vulgar or improper, in apples and stitches, in a uterus and an umbilical cord.

Airports pretend a certain veneer of sophistication, especially on Monday mornings when they're empty of tourists. They're the polar opposite of home, of the couch with our body shape moulded into the fabric, of the worn blanket that we keep out of the sight of guests. Flight attendant uniforms are the living embodiment of that veneer, outfits that are supposedly meant to cover up and clothe the attendants, but instead expose them and lay bare all the ceremony behind flight crew protocols. My book about the mother and son is the closest thing I can think of to a flight attendant's uniform.

Airports are also spaces on the margins of a story: they occur before anything has taken place or after everything has, preambles or epilogues where no one expects anything particularly noteworthy to happen. Lucía heads for the security line and I watch her drag her feet the whole way. I wave goodbye and walk back to the carpark. I drive to the music school with a renewed, furious joy. I park on the curb and an intense nausea washes over me, a mix of my new-found fury and the orange juice sloshing around in my stomach. I find a mint in the glove compartment that helps alleviate both and get out of the car, happy that I've managed to stand up without vomiting.

1
THE SECOND
CHILD

ALL MY MORNINGS WITH THE BOY BEGIN MORE OR LESS THE same way. He wakes up with his face and hair coated in a film of lethargy, though I couldn't say what it's made of, maybe because it's not made of anything tangible, or at least not something I can feel between my fingers. The film also coats his mouth, leaving it clumsy, and his words, sounding as if they've been reborn in their primitive forms. Unlike at bedtime, there's no urgency to the boy's words when he wakes up. He'll say something like "mama" or blubber some form of hello, random sounds devoid of meaning. The film even coats his hands and feet; I can see it in the way he grabs the teddies he sleeps with and the way he puts his feet on the floor. He walks through the hallway to the kitchen as if he's newly discovering the weight of his body and has to calculate, for the first time, the dimensions of the furniture and the height of the objects within reach. Then he drinks the glass of milk I've poured for him, and some mornings, he asks for another.

When the boy was a baby, the film was even thicker, and really did seem tangible. Something in the day would drain the freshness from his face and flatten his expression. By the end of any day, he went from being a child to being a chore, and the only things on my mind were the clothes to be picked up off the floor, the dishes to be washed, the fridge to be filled, and the care to be given to the boy, as if these were all equivalent tasks, chores to be checked off a list. His unique qualities as a human would be restored overnight, and every morning he was once again special purely for the fact of being alive. His skin took back its colour and elasticity, and his eyes their radiance. The boy is five years old now, and he's my son.

The boy makes some odd linguistic mistakes. He says 'cholcate,' instead of 'chocolate' and sometimes leaves his sentences unfinished, only to pick them back up, once he's ready, from the last syllable he uttered. For example, he might say: 'I'm gon ... and pause. Then he'll say '... na play with the wooden train.' He also gets colloquialisms wrong, so that when he tries to say that the girl in the story with the three bears is a 'liar, liar, pants on fire,' he says that she's a 'liar, liar ants on a wire.' I like the boy's defects and have never felt the need to correct them, but that's probably because I'm not the kind of mother I should be. The boy doesn't complain that he sleeps in dinosaur pyjama bottoms and an outer space top, or that I didn't take him for a haircut last week. Anytime it falls in front of his face while he's eating or drawing, he just brushes it aside with his chubby-fingered hand and moves on. The boy never complains about my defects because he doesn't know any other way for things to be.

For example, he didn't complain when I was a few minutes late picking him up from the music school on my way back from dropping Lucía at the airport. And the next morning, when I go to the school bus stop with him, he doesn't complain that I've forgotten to pack him the reusable water bottle he always takes to school. He brings it up, but delicately, downplaying the issue. I take him to a café and buy him a plastic bottle of water. He tells me that plastic is bad for the planet because it ends up in the sea and kills the fishes. I promise it won't happen again and apologise to him and to the fishes. He replies, full of sympathy, that it's no big deal. Then, he's on the bus and waving goodbye animatedly from the window, like I'm an utterly perfect mother.

After the boy leaves, I need to kill some time until the pharmacy opens, so I take a considerable detour through the university campus. I don't want to go to the pharmacy closest to me; I would rather trek to a neighbourhood where neither I nor anyone I know has ever lived and go to a mostly empty pharmacy the size of a supermarket. I remember exactly what temperature it was as I walked, the specific colours of the late-autumn sky, the brand of throat lozenges they had on sale, what clothes the people queuing wore, and what greetings and small talk we exchanged . I buy two tests there: one for pregnancy, one for ovulation.

Defining life events have the power to burn into our memory all the tiny, unnoticed things that happened right beforehand, like they're part of a natural ecosystem from which the spontaneous germinates. It's as if, despite having no direct relationship to what happened, they were somehow there to catalyse it, to draw a contrast, to reinforce the point—here's your shattered normalcy.

I'm sure that singular things do happen before, say, a devastating earthquake, but in stories about the precise moment when the earth split in two, no one describes how a couple was arguing loudly in the doorway to the post office, or how a man two streets up was violently stealing a motorbike. The scenes are always the same. People will say, 'I was reading the paper when it happened.' Or, 'I was walking to work, just like any other day, when suddenly.' All extraordinary days are extraordinary for precisely that reason: that before they became extraordinary, we expected them to slip into the indifferentiable mass of our regular days.

For the most part, we can't predict when something extraordinary is about to happen. The rare times that we can, our inkling of suspicion never matches up to our shock. The inkling can even serve to amplify it, the same way that preparing for a trip can increase our excitement at the prospect of discovering a new place. My inkling, though annoying, is small, easy to manage.

I'm not buying a pregnancy test and an ovulation test because I need them both. I'm buying them so the pharmacist will think I want to have a child, specifically, a second child. My theory is that if I buy a pregnancy test along with an ovulation test, she'll assume I'm trying to maximise my chances by determining my most fertile days and then she won't give me a nasty look. Pharmacists aren't exactly known for giving nasty looks to women who buy pregnancy tests, let alone making snide comments, but I can't bear the thought that a total stranger, even if she doesn't say it out loud, might think I'm buying the test because I've made some error of judgement whose prospects terrify me. Anyway, my strategy works. The pharmacist explains how to use an ovulation test and wishes me luck.

I listen patiently to her litany of instructions, though I already know how to use an ovulation test because I'd spent endless hours researching all the ways to increase my chances of pregnancy back when I was first trying to become a mother. Bringing the boy into the world wasn't easy, not some tender, loving adventure; it was a highly technical process. Through my research, I learned all sorts of things about the physiological changes that take place in my body for the duration of a cycle that has never lasted exactly twenty-eight days, or thirty, or twenty-six, for that matter. I can tell what's happening in my left ovary just by the texture of my cheeks.

I head home from the pharmacy with the two tests in a paper bag. Lucía messages me a rant about how her mother said that something or other about the wedding is over-the-top. I find myself thinking about rites of passage, about my son and the wedding, about the desire to grow up and lay claim to the symbols that set us apart from the adults we know, and the desire to argue with them over trivial things, allowing us to feel that we can both be our mothers and be nothing like them. About desire.

The desire for my first child came fully formed, the way we're led to believe it should. I imagined that having a child would bring me closer to a platonic ideal of happiness. I thought of a child as a wellspring. I wasn't unaware that motherhood brings its own set of challenges, or that raising a child is hard work, a monumental undertaking. My desire was neither frivolous nor uninformed, it was profound—at least I thought so—but I knew right from the start that the only way to muster the conviction necessary for something like that was to listen to the inner voice that says: 'Maybe it's not such a big deal.' I listened to that voice too much, I'm sure. So did Miguel, although he went a step further and fed into it with the earnest optimism of someone who's always done what he's supposed to, who has always followed the paths he's supposed to follow, successfully and without running into too many problems along the way.

I hadn't deluded myself into thinking that my love for my child would erase any problems that might arise. I was confident that I understood the challenges and had accepted them. For the most part, I thought of them as practical issues: fatigue, a new domestic routine, self-sacrifice, and surrendering my own time and pleasures, which I was more than willing to do.

When I was in college, I attended a lecture by a Bulgarian artist whose photos I found captivating. The photos were probably pretty (I don't remember them at all), but her lecture was a string of clichés about creation and fulfilment. At the beginning of her talk, she put a tall glass jar on the table and filled it up with rocks. She asked if we thought it was full. We all intoned a "yes," indulgently playing our assigned role. Then she picked up a jug full of water and poured it into the jar. Naturally, the water filled the empty spaces between the rocks. The artist said that we can never be too certain of total satisfaction. But that's how I thought about my child, as someone who would fill me with a happiness that could occupy all the empty spaces of my melancholy and boredom.

I once tried to write about the era that followed that desire for a child, a time that was, at first, happy and carefree, and later, oppressive. I made my calculations every month and waited for a pregnancy that never came. When it finally did, it came coupled with feelings of grief and failure, not to mention a vague diagnosis—recurrent pregnancy loss—which didn't seem like something that could be happening to me, because I was healthy and in my late twenties. In my first attempt to write about the experience, I clung to sarcasm and embraced shallowness in every single sentence, trying to debase myself so that the pipe-smoking reader would see that I, too, found the whole thing ridiculous, and that he would take pity on me. Not on me as a mother, but on me as a mother who wrote, and one who wrote as if her work were being produced by someone else, by someone who didn't see any particular value or literary merit in writing about a mother but simply couldn't resist the urge.

Contrary to the spontaneous urge to link writing and gestation—I instinctively dislike anyone who refers to books as children and writing as childbirth—I've never written more than I did after my first and second miscarriages, and never less than after I actually gave birth. Months before the boy had grown into a bulge in my belly, there had been another child. And another before that. A ten-week-old foetus is about the size of a grape, and a seven-week-old embryo, a seed. Yet I could have sworn that somehow, I knew the exact moment those conglomerations of cells ceased to be alive inside me, even though the first symptoms would take a few more days to appear.

Back home from my trip to the pharmacy, I share the lift with the old woman who lives on the eighth floor. She once told me that my mother was lucky I'd given her a grandson, because her daughters only cared about themselves. She also mentioned that she had a son who's a doctor, a dermatologist, to be specific. I don't know if that son has given her any grandchildren or not, but it seems evident that my eighth-floor neighbour doesn't have an issue with her son caring only about himself. I take the pregnancy test the moment I walk in the door, before removing my coat or boots, and leave it on the table in the living room. Within a few minutes, two coloured lines have appeared.

The paragraph originally ended there, but my friend Andrés said it might be a good idea for me to clarify whether two coloured lines signify a positive or negative result. At first, I considered mentioning here that this might not be a book for someone who doesn't know what it means when there are two coloured lines on a pregnancy test, but that wouldn't be true. What I can say is that it isn't a book for someone who thinks that two coloured lines on a pregnancy test are any less substantial than a war wound, a buried flag, or a fighter plane, or someone who expects me to replace apples and bananas with redcurrants and peaches.

I pick the boy up again at the bus stop at noon. Children's routines are like circles that enclose their adults' time into segments of obligation. He's in a good mood, his hair is messy, and his cheeks are red, like they always are when he comes back from school.

We walk through the park by our house and I ask if he's hungry. He asks me to listen to the sound of his footsteps on the leaves, which still litter the path even though it's December and the municipal workers usually clear them every couple of weeks. The boy says that his footsteps sound like growls, like nice leaf growls.

The boy inhabits the realm of metaphor. He devotes himself to it; he invents the language and the properties of the objects, which are almost always alive when he names them. He stuffs it all together in his jacket pockets: the metaphors alongside the variously-sized rocks he picks up off the ground, the names of things alongside the small balls of playdough he steals from school, and the difficult words alongside the colourful figurines he likes to collect, which are made of plastic, though in this case, he doesn't seem to mind.

2
COMMON
VIPER

EVERY SO OFTEN I SKETCH ARCHITECTURE. FOR EXAMPLE, I'LL sit in Praza de San Roque—on one of those benches with flaking green paint, in front of the tall trees with flaking bark, after they've lost all their leaves and winter is near (always at that time of year)—and sketch the corner of a building: its signs of deterioration, its labyrinth of pipes, its electrical boxes, and event posters.

I sketch homes because homes, unlike people, stay still, but I write about people precisely because they're in motion. If I had to say one thing about the people in my books, I wouldn't discuss the characters, I would discuss the friends who prop them up. Their discreet readings, their provisional marks on the page, used to be invisible. Now, I leave them in plain sight; I want to display them, to accord them their rightful place, which is that of the pipes, the electrical boxes, and the event posters. They come and go from the narrative without a sound and, like the electrical cables in a sketch of a building, they don't hold any greater meaning within it. Yet, it's those cables that bring light into people's homes. Friends do something of the sort for novels.

I call Mónica a few hours after I see the two lines on the pregnancy test. I think she's exactly the switch I need to flip, because she lives far away—ideal for telling uncomfortable secrets to—and because she's a nurse. We usually talk at least a couple of times a month, and text each other often. We rarely see each other face-to-face, but I think that's fine. The few times we do get together in-person, we make the small effort to break away from the strictures of our disembodied conversations, because we know it's the only way to sustain them. We'll say, 'Can't wait to see you,' or, 'It's too bad you can't come on holiday this year,' but we don't mean it. Mónica listens in silence while I ask about the procedure for a voluntary termination—that's the exact expression I use— and what she thinks I should do.

I told Carlos in a few sentences, and cold ones, I'm sure, as soon as he came home. We were in the kitchen, and I didn't ask him to sit down, meanwhile the boy was playing with building blocks on the rug in the living room. No fissure appeared between us, not that I'd expected to find one, and because I gave no indication that I saw this as anything but an annoyance, let alone something that was going to re-arrange our lives, he immediately banished words like child and pregnancy, and began to refer to it as *the situation*.

One thing I've always appreciated about Mónica is her knack for asking questions that don't force you to explain further or talk about something you might not want to. I didn't have to tell her that I felt neither lucky due to this unexpected pregnancy, nor guilty for not wanting a second child.

I had some ideas about abortion, about the timelines and legal guarantees, and also a fear, irrational or not, of being forced to defend myself against other people's ideas. If imagining the disapproving look of a random pharmacist was enough to make me uneasy, the thought of disappointing or wounding the people that love me, particularly my grandmother María, was enough to push me over the edge. I started constructing detailed and utterly implausible scenarios, playing them out in my head like I was plotting a novel. In the worst scenes, I imagined preposterous coincidences like going to a public hospital at exactly the same day and time as my grandmother María has an appointment with the eye doctor, whose office is, of course, right next door to the obstetrician, a man who won't meet my eyes (it's always a man in these fantasies) and whose white coat is pinned with a badge proclaiming that he's the abortionist, only for him to call my first and last names out in a voice so loud that everyone in the vicinity can hear him, inviting me to come in, and then commenting, still loudly and in public, on *the situation.*

I had too many ideas, and they all swirled around in my head among all the other thoughts in an unstoppable vortex, like a flock of starlings when they form a vague blotch that swells and contracts in the sky. I also had too many melancholies, all more or less intact from the time when I was trying to become a mother, only for the embryos to dissipate or fall away from my endometrial tissue as if they'd inherited my detached personality from the very moment of their inception as cells. I assumed that my grandmother María would find *the situation* appalling, and that if she found out about it, I would forever lose her as a source of compassion and comfort. It didn't matter that she wasn't very lucid anymore, or that there was almost no way she would ever find out: nothing could stop my obfuscations.

My first pregnancy was ectopic. The embryo had developed near my right ovary, which led to moderate bleeding. I was in the hospital for a week without understanding what that actually meant at first. They had to remove my ovary and fallopian tube. I woke from the anaesthetic in a cold room, clutching at the metal rails of the bed as I struggled to sit up.

My entire family found out. My grandmother María was the only one who didn't tell me the embryo was an angel, or a star watching over me in the heaven for dead babies. All she asked was what they did with the undeveloped babies and their bodies after an abortion. I think she might have even said the word *corpse*. It gave the tiny embryos and their beating hearts the air of defective babies. My grandmother María has always dragged her sorrow around with her to someplace where she can learn the practical consequences of things. Once she has, she then focuses on finding solutions to what's solvable, and to understanding what's not. I told her that the embryo was about the size of a grain of rice and that it didn't make sense to ask what they'd done with the body, because, strictly speaking, there was none. My uncle Pedro only wanted to know whether they'd *emptied* me during the operation, taking for granted that I would understand what the word meant, and that my uterus could be simultaneously useless and the only organ that determined whether or not I was whole.

When I talk to Mónica, some more violent words join that troop of lexical phantoms alongside the concept of emptied women. She gives me the number of a private clinic which is, conveniently, both discreet and far from my home; she tells me to call and make an appointment. Before I call, I scour the web for information on timelines and types of voluntary termination, on prices and common procedures. At one point, the word *scrape* comes up, and I envision my body as a vessel encrusted with a filth that will have to be removed by some unholy looking instrument.

All the women I knew who'd been emptied or scraped, or those who'd lost their children, were victims. Those terms denoted a state of the body that couldn't help but provoke the pity of respectable people like my uncle Pedro. They were waterless jugs, broken vases, dried husks. To my uncle Pedro, they were the 'poor little things.' They were half-women, or stained women, but at least they weren't bad women. Women who'd been emptied got to keep their reputations because they were free from blame.

No one was more free from blame than Belinda, who was a part of the landscape in those Augusts we spent at my grandparents' summer house. Her house was blue and next-door to ours, which was white. Belinda's father kept a row-boat in their yard. She would let me climb into it sometimes so that I could pretend I was a captain or a pirate in the midst of a violent storm. Her name had a haughty, vivacious ring to my ears. She had big eyes and always wore her long hair loose. The summer when I was nine, she also had a child in her belly. All the adults wished her 'a smooth delivery' and asked when the baby was going to come. She would smile broadly and say, 'the bun's almost ready,' and that it would come at any moment, as soon as it was ready.

That phrase, 'the bun's almost ready,' stuck to the roof of my mouth, because Belinda's child was stillborn and she had to have a hysterectomy. I never played with her again. I don't think I ever saw her again, either, or at least that's what I wrote here at first when I was trying to tell the story. My mother later told me that we kept seeing Belinda every year and that she actually still lives there, in the same blue house. I guess emptied women also become invisible, disappear from the centre; the group pushes them so far away from their little girls and their happiness that they're exiled from people's memories, above all, the memories of those women who are still whole.

My grandparents' summer home had two floors. My sister and I slept on the second floor in a room with bunk beds, a round table, and a window covered with metal bars. The beds were covered in green linen bedspreads with tassels, the table a white tablecloth, and the window a set of thick curtains my grandmother María would close every day at noon, when the sunlight began to pour through. Every piece of furniture in that house ended up covered in some sort of fabric. There were crochet cloths on top of the sofa headrests and every side table, and runners on top of the credenza in the hall and the dressers that held the sheets and towels in my parents' room. In my family, everything is concealed, covered up, and shielded from the casual glance.

Anyway, none of that exists anymore. The furniture was all sold or given away, the house had new owners for a few years, and not long after that, it was demolished. Someone built a bigger house in its place. I don't know if it's prettier or more modern because I haven't been back.

In the backyard, there was a hortensia bush where my father once killed a common viper which was lying motionless on the cement path that surrounded our house. I was upset that morning because the doll I played mommy with wasn't where I'd left it the day before. To be fair, it was my only doll and I didn't enjoy playing mommy all that much. I had left it in the sun to let its hair dry after I'd given it a bath in the fountain. I cried over its disappearance with little conviction and called it *my baby*. My grandmother María promised to buy me a new one and took me into town, where I picked out a white basket and a bell for my bicycle. That's why I didn't see the viper. My sister told me the story that night as we lay in our bunk beds, she on the bottom one and me on the top, unable to see each other's faces, like my conversations with Mónica. With the muffled sounds of the adults having dinner downstairs, my sister provided me with all sorts of powerful details.

She told me that the viper was pregnant and that there were tiny snakes coming out of a hole in its body. I said that was impossible because snakes lay eggs, but she swore it was true, and it was: common vipers do give birth to their offspring. She told me they looked like translucent gelatin fingers covered in webs of blood. I imagined them as a gooey hand—not a group of bodies but a single entity whose every part was a continuation of the other, like the image of a snake biting its own tail as a representation of something that never ends.

The viper had slithered out from underneath our hortensia bush, and I haven't gone near one since. I think I'm still afraid of them. That's probably why I noticed the hortensia petal that fell off Lucía's wedding crown at the airport, like a hazy apparition from the past, or a premonition of the future.

I call the clinic half an hour before they close. While I speak with the woman on the other end, who doesn't identify herself—I'm not sure if she's a receptionist or part of the medical staff, though I assume the first—I doodle in my planner with a pen. I draw snakes and flowers, which are really just groups of lines and circles, because I don't know how to draw snakes or flowers that would be easily recognisable as such.

I mentioned earlier that I sketch buildings because they stay still, but I almost never draw trees, even though they don't move so fast that they would change posture in the time it would take me to sketch them. Living things are imprinted with life in a way that's hard to convey on paper. Trees incline their leaves towards the light. If you sketch a tree, you can't angle the branches however you'd like, or however you remember them, because it's their directionality that tells you they're alive and are conditioned by change, though that conditioning has less to do with the way the wind blows or what human beings do to their bark, and more with an internal movement. I never sketch life, because it's self-sufficient and ever-shifting. But I do sketch vehicles, statues, parabolic antennae on roofs: what someone else has put somewhere, but never what has grown.

I always, and only, sketch what's sterile.

3
THAT PLACE

THE RECEPTIONIST EXPLAINS THE PROCEDURE WITHOUT pausing, as if she doesn't need to search for the words, just remember them. The only interruptions to her monologue which make it possible to differentiate her voice from a recording, are my questions. First, I'll have to go to the clinic for a preliminary consultation, where they'll perform an ultrasound and determine how long I've been pregnant. I don't need to worry, because from the sound of it, I'm not very far along yet, maybe five or six weeks.

The next step is to pick an option. Prior to seven weeks, a pregnancy can be terminated pharmaceutically. They would give me a pill, which I could swallow right there in the clinic, and then another that I'd have to insert like a tampon at home the next day. That's the simplest option, she says, but it also has certain consequences: guaranteed heavy bleeding, as well as severe cramps, which they then treat with painkillers. She doesn't say 'consequences'—I think— instead using a more neutral expression like 'side effects' or something along those lines. My body would do all the work.

The other option would be for them to take charge. I would make an appointment for an operation under local anaesthetic where they would dilate my cervix, insert a narrow tube, and proceed to vacuum out the embryonic tissue. In this scenario I would have to stay at the clinic for a few hours to recover from the anaesthetic or sedative. I might have some discomfort for a few days afterwards. If I'd felt guilty, I think this would have seemed like insufficient punishment.

The receptionist says that most women choose the first option if they can. For one, because it's less invasive, but also because it has a higher success rate with early-stage pregnancies. I'd guess they also opt for this route because it's more private, and maybe because they imagine their grandmothers happening to walk down the exact street where the clinic is, confusing it with their laundrette, and wandering into the clinic and through the hall in a muddle—of course, no one stopping them—while they look for a duvet or a coat with a coffee stain on the collar, only to stumble upon their granddaughters asleep with their legs spread.

The receptionist also tells me how much each option costs, which can vary depending upon the type of anaesthetic you choose. Again, she doesn't use the word 'cost;' she says 'rate,' the same way she didn't say 'consequences,' but 'side effects.' Carlos and I begin to discuss our options for the situation and their corresponding rates and side effects, adopting the language of the clinic because it's the most effective at covering up the facts.

I decide on the second option: whatever is quickest and requires the least involvement from me. When I tell Carlos, he nods without showing any surprise. I'm annoyed to find no flaws in his conduct, no thoughtlessness. He's stepped into the role of a man who knows he shouldn't interfere in choices that affect a body which isn't his, and stands by whatever decision I make, but he does it with too much tact, like he's been trained, like it's a matter of protocol.

I'm also annoyed that my appointment for the preliminary consultation won't be until Friday, because that means I'll have to wait until next week for the operation. They assure me that they'll do everything in their power to schedule my operation for next Monday or Tuesday, at the latest, so I can get it all over with. I do the maths and realise that, between the operation and the post-op visit, the process won't be finalised until after Christmas, and I yearn for the days to be shorter than they are. When I look back on it now, they could have hardly handled it with more grace and diligence, and I could hardly have asked for greater efficiency. Still, it was one of the longest weeks of my life. Every morning, my son would remove a surprise chocolate from his advent calendar, and I would glare at my own with an agitation not dissimilar to his.

I dream about labour multiple nights in a row. Sometimes it's me in labour, others it's someone else and I'm just there, for no obvious reason. In two of the dreams, the child is born in an intact amniotic sac. Caul births, or 'veiled births,' as we call them, are extremely rare, but they often appear in books about pregnancy because there's something special, something beautiful about these odd occurrences. The name itself is fascinating: caul comes from the Latin for 'head-dress,' and our term, 'veiled birth,' seems to convey a similar idea. It gestures at some sort of protection or secrecy, at an ancient magic. It's often said that caul babies are born with good luck, that they're protected from drowning or bestowed with extraordinary powers. But it's become commonplace in hospital births for the sac to be artificially popped with a medical instrument: it speeds up the process.

Five years earlier, I felt the sudden, impetuous burst of the sac in my womb a few hours before I went into labour. I was in the kitchen cooking. I remember feeling cheated. The child hadn't yet taken a concrete form in my mind, despite its eager movements inside me and the moments when I could make out a hand or a foot through the contorted skin of my stomach. I took a shower, and the warm, gleaming amniotic fluid continued to flow and flow while the water washed over me. The sun was tentative that day. What I mean is that it was an unusual season for the sun to be out, so you couldn't help but feel the good weather was liable to disappear at any moment, or that it was a deceptive gift. The apartment where I lived with Miguel had a well-lit terrace, and through the bathroom window, to the left of the shower, all the light from that terrace, tinged with the colours of the flowers and plants, poured good cheer through the glass.

Miguel dropped me off at the hospital entrance while he parked the car. At reception, they asked if I was alone and wanted to call anyone. I thought about how I'd never be alone again, how from that point on I would always be with my son and he with me, and I didn't want anyone else at my side because my baby was all I needed. I nearly forgot that Miguel would be back in a matter of minutes to shatter my bold, emphatic solitude. There was no room in my mind for misgivings or fears about going into labour, only a radiant power, a brazen desire.

I remember thinking all these things as if they were true, with a genuine joy that dissolved in a matter of hours, like snow that never manages to lay, mixing with the dirt and grime of the pavement until it turns into something no one wants to look at. Over the course of the hours it took for my soon to be born, it was hard not to notice that the nurses and gynaecologist acted as if I didn't exist. They had started to refer to me without using my name, and never directly addressed me. When they needed to communicate to each other about me, they always called me 'the mother.' It wasn't just my son that had left my body that day, but also, and above all, me; over the course of a few hours, I had ceased to be myself and had become 'the mother.' 'The mother is doing a good job collaborating with us,' the midwife had said when the baby was crowning. As if the mother had any other choice.

There's a note on the hospital report explaining that they'd had to induce labour, but no one had said a word to me about it. My contractions started at two in the afternoon as a minor pain. Four hours later, my son was lying on my chest and I was in a daze trying to get the feeling back in my feet, still strapped into stirrups in the hospital bed. It was like there were ants crawling all over them. My body was some territory that didn't belong to me. From my spot on the bed, I could see the ceiling and the eyes of all the people around me, the tubes pumping saline solution through my arm, and the sterile blue or green hospital blanket draped over my knees. I tried to recall, or put an order to, some of the events of the past few hours, like the entrance of the anesthesiologist who had given me the epidural. He had snapped for me to hold still, for my own good, and to stop fussing, like I was some frivolous girl who needed to be put in her place.

Whatever joy I'd felt before, not only upon my arrival at the hospital, but at any point in my life, morphed, with the baby's birth, into a quiet estrangement. I found myself unable to share in his father's excitement, or to register the staff's congratulations when they were addressed to me.

In reality, they weren't. They were addressed to 'the mother,' that other person I'd suddenly become. Apparently my months of pregnancy hadn't been sufficient warning of what was to come. It was perplexing to hear them call me that, and although at first it was something others referred to me as, I quickly accepted it as inevitable and started to refer to myself that way, too, miming a role that didn't feel natural to me. Anytime someone said my son's name as shorthand for the both of us, like in the waiting room at the paediatrician's, I would raise my hand. 'Are you the mother?' some faceless nurse would ask, and I would say yes—never, 'Yes, that's me,' only 'Yes'—because I no longer was me, I was 'the mother.'

My son looked just like any other small, non-human mammal. It had never occurred to me that this might be the case

until the moment he was born. He was a few weeks prema-
ture, and for the first couple hours, I gazed in horror upon
his tiny, five-pound body, covered in a soft, fine fur that took
a while to disappear completely. His skin was yellow at first,
more like a lemon than an egg yolk. The midwife told me
that lots of babies are born with jaundice, that lots of babies
are born with hair on their bodies, and above all, that lots of
babies are born prematurely, which means they're only half-
done. The technical terms provided no comfort. 'You don't
need to worry about him,' she said.

I wasn't worried. Not about him. I said I didn't want to
breastfeed. Without any questions, they brought me two
white pills that I was meant to take together to stop my
breasts from producing milk. I took them, I think, with a
sense of optimism.

I'm not sure why I didn't want to breastfeed. At the same
time as I simulated feeling the way I was supposed to, ex-
claiming to my visitors how happy this perfect little boy had
made me, I also felt an urgent need to put myself as far as
possible away from my mother-body in the hopes of moving
closer to my body from before. A night nurse brought me a
toylike bottle filled with baby formula. She told me, like it
was a secret or something she shouldn't tell me but was true,
that I was doing the right thing, because breastfeeding was
a misery and children grew up no differently without it,
contradicting all scientific evidence to the contrary.
Afterwards, I plunged into a deep sleep and Miguel took over
looking after our son, tending to him when he cried and

feeding him when it was time. I woke up at sunrise. The same nurse who'd spoken approvingly of my decisions as a mother the night before glared at me from the hallway with an undisguised contempt, I guess because of the selflessness I wasn't bothering to feign.

Despite my precautions, only two days later, back at home, I felt some oily drops of milk leaking from my left breast, dampening my shirt. I also felt a pain that reminded me of other kinds of pain, without being quite like anything I'd felt before. My breasts had turned hard, rebellious: my body was a land under bombardment. I got used to finding large blood clots like chicken livers in my underwear, and to wrapping my breasts in chest binders that I stuffed with bags of frozen vegetables, which would quickly thaw out.

It takes nine months for a child to form in the womb and be born, but no one knows how long it takes for a mother to do the same. Not the mother that particular child needs, but the mother that woman wants to be. After giving birth, I had no interest in hearing other mothers talk about their babies' diets, paediatric goals, or swimming lessons. What I wanted was for them to tell me how they'd forgiven their children for dismantling the women they'd been. It wasn't enough for me to know that, in some peculiar way, I loved my baby. I needed to understand why, maybe because I thought that could change things. But the women in the waiting rooms never talked about their children, and I never talked about my son. I never talked at all.

A new mother is a woman grieving for the woman she has left behind. But it's a grief that receives no consolation. Instead, it's buried under piles of new dresses and tiny clothes with lace ribbons. No other change in life demands so much in return, or, even more than that, so much silence. When someone leaves their country because they've accepted an exciting new job on the other side of the world, it comes as no surprise to learn that whatever joy or excitement they might feel is also tinged with uncertainty and nostalgia. That's never the case with a recent mother. A new mother is a place without room for controversy or regret, meant to be wholly occupied by happiness.

And I don't want to go back to that place.

4
A GIFT

I VISIT MY GRANDMOTHER MARÍA ON ONE OF THE DAYS BEFORE my first appointment at the clinic, just after lunch. I choose that time of day because I think she tends to be more lucid. Before I go in, I notice the camellias on the path around my grandparents' house. They have two types of camellias: white and pink. The white camellias bloom earlier, in mid-December. My grandfather told me that years ago, and repeated it again to me at some point before he died, so I remember it every time I see them. I'm not sure why, but it's always in my mind.

My grandparents' house is on top of a hill in the upper part of the city. After they bought the land, they took me to see it on Saint María's day. My father used a heavy stone to draw a rectangle marking out the place where they would build their house as a way to help me imagine it, and I understood that this place was also for me. They brought a folding table and an umbrella, and we ate lunch together, mussels with lemon and a salad. That night, we watched the holiday fireworks in the sky above the neighbourhood. They wrapped me in a big coat of my aunt's, who was sixteen at the time. I stuffed my hands into the pockets and found a lighter inside. It was also for me not to tell the adults that my aunt had a lighter in her coat pocket.

After they built the house, they got together to dig a hole to one side of it so that they could install a circular pool. They made a human chain, scooping out buckets of dirt and passing them out of the hole. I don't know how many days they spent working on it. But I remember when the pool came; it was a rigid basin with a blue interior. I swam wearing a rubber ring with a swan's neck while my aunts, uncles, and parents sunbathed in their hammocks, watching me. I'd always been afraid of water, but knowing they were all there, watching me, was enough for me to feel safe.

My grandmother is sitting in the most comfortable armchair in the living room, beside the wheelchair she uses to get around with the help of my uncle Pedro, who lives with her and is her daily caretaker. I kiss her on the head and tell her the thing about the camellias, but she shows no interest. She asks me what day it is. Sometimes, these questions are like the railings my uncle put up in the hallway when my grandmother could still walk. She uses the answers to manoeuvre through the conversation: what day is it today, what time is it now. I tell her it's Thursday and she asks me the day of the month and how soon it is until my father's birthday, which falls shortly before Christmas.

Then she tells me what it was like giving birth to my father, her firstborn. When the pains started, she didn't quite know what they meant. She wasn't sure that she was going into labour. As if everything were normal, she went to the lot where she hung clothes out to dry. And she hung them, I think. Then she went home and didn't have time to call anyone. The baby was born without the help of a midwife, without any company. When she talks about her first birth, she speaks fondly about the baby. He was tiny, 'he looked like a little monkey when he was born.' We've rarely discussed these kinds of things before, and the topic couldn't feel more inopportune.

She also tells me about my uncle Pedro, who was born with a dislocated arm. She tells me how delicate he was, how special. She tells me what my aunt was like when she was little: sharp and determined, rambunctious. She tells me about my youngest uncle, the only one of her children born in a hospital, and how they sewed her up after she gave birth and she realised that she had endured reparable wounds from her previous childbirths for years: 'That's how it used to be.' She has a precise adjective for each child, one that still explains who they are to this day. My grandmother María has comprehended something about her children that slipped through my fingers when my own son was born. Somehow, she knew the moment they came out of her why she loved her children so much, and I didn't.

When my aunt died, on a bright afternoon like this one, my grandmother was waiting to hear the worst from the hospital while she sat silently in the kitchen. It was the last day of many months of illness and deterioration, but we didn't know that yet. I had gone to see my grandmother a few hours before it happened, entering the house through the balcony door, from the garden. We usually used the garage door, but that day she had flung open all the doors and windows and there were draughts of air gusting through the halls and rooms, like the whole house was a heart, open to the inclemencies of the weather, a heart that couldn't contain itself, that had let itself go, or abandoned all hope of self-protection. That day, too, I noticed the camellias outside; they were starting to fall. Camellias are the only flower that don't break apart when they fall, which happens just before spring, while everything else around them is starting to bloom. The house was freezing, which was unusual, and my grandmother was wearing a green winter housecoat, which was the norm. This was many years ago, when she could still walk unaided. 'I'll never heal from this grief.' As time went on, her sadness grew more profound, more silent. That's how my grandmother thinks she has to dignify her sorrow.

Ever since my aunt died my grandmother María has started to give her things away as soon as an opportunity arises; she wants to say goodbye to us every day, as if all the time she's alive is time she shouldn't have, time past her date. She asks me to open one of her dresser drawers and pick something out from inside it, whatever I want: a bracelet, a statue of the Virgin Mary, a ring, anything that belongs to her. It frustrates me again to see her trying to say a definitive goodbye. I've never handled definitive endings well, it's as if there's something obscene in accepting them, but what's more obscene is refuting the knowledge that my loved ones are mortal.

When he was ninety-four, one of my father's uncles went in for a minor surgery to replace the battery in his pacemaker. The surgeon said the batteries lasted for a decade, so my father told him he wouldn't have to worry about it until the next procedure, as if it were only polite to assume there would be one ten years later, and rude to suggest otherwise. He died at ninety-six, before that could happen, as anyone would have expected.

Grandma María insists that I'm her first granddaughter and that she no longer has a daughter, while I peel an apple for her to eat in the middle of the afternoon. She asks me where the baby is, what I've done with him. The question leaves our conversation hanging in the air for a few seconds while I freeze with the knife in one hand, the half-peeled fruit in the other. Obviously, I think about the pregnancy test, the call to the clinic, and my constant panic at being discovered. In spite of all that, I manage to separate the imaginary from the improbable and tell her a few things about my son, on the assumption that it's him she's referring to, and that she's lost all notion of how old he is.

She's actually asking about my father. I realise immediately. I understand that none of what I'm saying about my son is, to her, a valid response, and she wants to know where that other baby is, her baby. I can also tell she's able to grasp that I'm her granddaughter, at the same time as she believes there's also a baby she loves and cares for that exists somewhere in the present, as if she's been left with an old but still vivid memory of that period of her life.

My uncle Pedro explains to me afterwards that my grandmother often talks about taking care of a little boy. The hospital neurologist has recommended we buy her a doll to take care of; supposedly it can be comforting or beneficial for people who have lost their grip on time or reality. He hands me a piece of paper where he's written the address of a website that sells—for astronomical prices—hyper-realistic dolls, like the kind they use in films. The premise horrifies me, but I promise him I'll look into it, so I can fulfil my grandmother's wish for a vessel which she can fill with her fond memories.

After tea, Uncle Pedro and I help her wash her hands in the bathroom. My grandmother María has certain obligatory rituals, which are numerous, very precise, and for the most part, pleasant. My uncle tries to respect all of the quirks and routines she has accumulated over the years, although he never gets them all quite right. When my grandmother could move around on her own, she would comb the tassels on the rugs a few times a day and run her hand along the surface so that all the threads of wool were facing the same direction. Even now, immediately after she washes her hands while in the wheelchair, she meticulously cleans the sink as best she can. She keeps a hand towel placed there to dry her hands with, a pretty towel to cover the hand towel, and a linen cloth, almost always pink, so that she can wipe away the drops that have been left behind after turning on the tap. She can't stand leaving traces.

Decency is important to her. For my grandmother María, being decent comes down to two things: most of all, cleanliness, but also the idea that there's a right way to do everything. She keeps sets of underwear and nightgowns that she's never worn, just in case she has to go to the hospital, and she's loyal to one brand of detergent. She suffers with every change and hates losing control. Her pantry is well-stocked with products of all kinds: six packets of rice, two bottles of fabric softener, everything prepared so that she will never, at any moment, be left wanting.

Conversations with my grandmother María generally revolve around one of two topics. She likes to talk about the novelties that make her daily life interesting: 'The cherry tree blossomed.' 'Your uncle brought toffee.' She also likes to talk about scarcity, about the contrasts between daily life back then and daily life now. Whenever she tries to tell you something about her life back then, she explains it by telling you what there wasn't: 'There was no television.' 'There was no toffee.' And she explains it like it's impossible to convey, like it's not enough for her to enumerate all the things she didn't have for us to truly understand what it meant not to have them.

As a girl I loved it when she told stories about being my age. She was born in a tiny house with a dirt floor. She once told me that she didn't have a bathroom or running water until she was married. She didn't have more than a couple pairs of shoes back then, either, and would only wear one pair on special occasions. As a teenager, she wore slippers everywhere. Whenever she walked into the city, she carried her shoes in her hand and only put them on once she was downtown. Before her teens, she went everywhere barefoot. The ladies would gape at her bare feet, and one woman told her it was a shame for such a pretty girl to be so dirty and gave her a coin. She has always been generous with tips, gifts for children, food, and invitations. She has always offered what she has to give, and has always done so without any great fanfare. She taught me the names of the best flowers to give other people: never roses (because they're presumptuous), ideally something with value that doesn't call too much attention to itself, like tulips, which are pretty but not obtrusive. She has always found the stinginess of those with money to be the worst of flaws, but she has no love of ostentation either.

Maybe this is why, while I wash her hands, she offers me a lavender-scented decorative soap by the sink, because she's not going to use it anymore. She tells me to take it home, or give it to the boy, it's shaped like a dolphin and she's sure he'll like it because children like such things. She tries to convince me to do her this favour, she says that the soap bothers her just sitting there, that she really bought it for me, even though it's been in the same place for twenty years. Uncle Pedro gives me a look of resignation, like he's trying to say this is how she is and I shouldn't pay her any mind. I tell her I'll bring the boy one day so she can give him the soap herself, and I return to the camellias that have blossomed and the December cold. Soon afterwards, we say goodbye.

I catch a bus to the lower part of the city and walk home in no particular hurry. No one is waiting for me. Carlos is working on the set of a show that's filmed in a town by the coast. He was contacted a week ago by a production company where someone knew him tangentially, from something else, to ask if he would coach the lead actresses on the local accent. Some of their scenes are set at night on the beach, so he won't be back until dawn. The boy is at his father's place, most likely eating dinner or already in bed. I'm surprised to see Christmas lights at the mall in the distance, which reminds me that I have to buy Lucía a wedding present, and that I can't put it off any longer.

At home, I fall onto the living room couch and have a bowl of soup that was left in the fridge, like I've just returned from a trip. Maybe I have. I open my laptop and look for a train ticket to Madrid for Lucía's wedding on the thirty-first of December. Then, I type in the address and password for the virtual gift registry and pick out a small household appliance that fits my budget. I write a short message with my best wishes for the happy couple, though I know that they would exchange all of those wedding gifts—and maybe even those best wishes—for anything else.

Finally, I visit the webpage for the hyper-realistic dolls that were recommended by the neurologist. The succession of photos of silicone babies horrifies me. On one side of the page, they have information about the therapeutic benefits of the dolls, but most of the people who buy them have a different purpose in mind. In the best of cases, collection. In the most disturbing, play. I once saw a report in the Extremadura news where they interviewed a woman who had three. She took one with her wherever she went, buying it clothes at children's fashion stores. She detailed all the morning and nightly routines she followed with them, under the pretence that they were real children. She never referred to them as objects or something she'd acquired, and only used the names she'd chosen when she *adopted* them.

The woman in the report had two daughters, one was a teenager and the other nine years old. Neither of them participated in their mother's game, but they seemed happy and unbothered by the situation.

The company recommended by the neurologist has gone to great lengths to convey a neutral, civilised appearance on their website, and they focus solely on the uses for the dolls that I imagine are the easiest for the average person to accept. The catalogue makes note of the meticulously painted imperfections in the dolls' skin, the softness of the plastic, the painstaking handmade process, the shape of the hands, the anatomical positioning of the arms and bent head, the weight, and the expressions. The images are indistinguishable from a modern-day photo of a real baby.

I pick out the one that looks the nicest and least scary, and after making the payment, an automated email tells me it will arrive within a week. It's also possible to order a doll that looks like a specific child—an existing child—by providing one or more photographs. For that, there's a nine-month waiting list. The process seems disturbing to me, but I decide that I probably shouldn't give it too much thought and make it my Christmas present for Grandma María, even though I'm not sure Grandma María will know Christmas when it comes.

5
SUPERTRAMP

PRIVATE ABORTION CLINICS BEAR A STRIKING RESEMBLANCE to private fertility clinics. They're only visited by people with a delicate imperfection, one they wouldn't readily confess to either strangers or loved ones, and they both look like fake medical offices, with that false sense of welcome. In private fertility clinics, there are photos hanging on the walls: laughing women and serene landscapes, or laughing women in serene landscapes, almost always accompanied by beautiful babies with pink skin, which look like they're straight out of the catalogue of silicone babies where I picked out the one for my grandmother María. The couches are white and the furniture is made of a light-coloured wood.

Nothing is white in the other clinics. There are no transparent panels, no atmosphere of purity, the walls are decorated in solid colours—black, green—and you can hide behind opaque glass. There's decoration suited to sympathy and decoration suited to indulgence. But they do share one definitive trait: that office-like style, the feeling that the scenery is as important as the scene, something which I've never felt in a public hospital. The distance between the place where the good mothers and the guilty mothers wait is curt and ambiguous.

I attend my first abortion appointment with Carlos, the way five years earlier I went to a fertility clinic with Miguel in search of an explanation for what was happening to us after the second miscarriage, still with the desire to have a child, which seemed impossible to give up on at the time. The one uneasiness is twinned with the other, though the impatience manifests differently. In both instances, my appointment is on a Friday.

The gynaecologist who sees me now is also reminiscent of the one who saw me five years ago. Both tell me the exact same thing: that I'm in the right place and that they have lots of experience helping women like me. I think the body language of the second might be more reserved, the inflection of her sentences more formal, her coat a little less white, and her office not as bright. She performs a quick ultrasound and confirms the timeline of the pregnancy—six weeks and six days—then tries to convince me, quite dispassionately, that abortion pills are less invasive and that I'm still in the window of time where I can put an end to all of this naturally, at home: the limit is seven weeks, as they'd said over the phone. Finally, she makes an appointment for me, for after the weekend, for the second option, on the twenty-first of December, ten days before Lucía's wedding.

At the fertility clinic, they also used words like help or option, but back then I'd interpreted them as jargon intended to dull the sharp edges of a sad situation. The same words, when applied to abortion, appear to function as a way of avoiding the shameful naming of each and every thing. None of the women in the waiting room has anyone with them except for me. The other two are alone, not meeting anyone's eyes, and Carlos is an intruder, an anomaly. I don't remember this being the case for Miguel five years ago. At the other clinic, there were often couples waiting together, and some had brought their other babies with them. The rest of the patients—me included—would look at the couples who already had children with suspicion. I considered them greedy; it wasn't enough for them to have one healthy bouncing baby, they wanted another, one I didn't think they deserved, because it only seemed fair to believe in the equitable distribution of babies.

Yet, once my son was born, those greedy mothers seemed infinitely superior to me. Not only had they joyously welcomed the arrival of their babies, they had also meshed perfectly into that precise image of fulfilment and dedication, and were ready to repeat the process even though they knew what it entailed. They were like the radiant mother who, one day, seeing me with the boy in my baby carrier at the library, told me that she had three of her own at home—five, eight, and twelve—and that she'd have even more if she could, that she would spend her whole life raising children because nothing in the world could compare to that satisfaction. It made me feel sad, or guilty, that she'd chosen those words to try and create an intimacy with me. I admit that I judged her, the way I judged all good mothers. I wasn't able to recognise the layers beneath everything they did and said, because I viewed them solely through the distorted lens of my own experience.

After the appointment, Carlos and I drive home on the motorway and talk. I almost added animatedly, but that's not quite accurate. I'm reminded of those other trips with Miguel to the fertility clinic, both of us silent, watching the electrical cables pass by through the car windows. Maybe we were losing our love for each other and that's why we didn't say much. Later, after the boy was born, we said even less, and it became obvious to us that there was a problem, even if it was hard to put our fingers on what. Letting each other go had been as simple as meeting at that party, as if we knew from the beginning that there would be an end and as if, over those past few years, we were simply waiting for it to come, not so different from knowing the tulip in a vase is going to die before long: you watch it deteriorate in the water until the day comes when you can't put off getting rid of it any longer, and have to move onto something else, grateful for the time when it was beautiful.

There are rarely silences between Carlos and me. He always finds something to say. He tells me about the first time he saw snow, and some stories from the set of the TV show he's working on. I put on a Supertramp CD, specifically, Crisis? What Crisis?, which opens with someone whistling. I don't want the drive to end because the inertia of moving from place to place has always been a balm for me. For the first few months of my son's life, when I didn't know what else to do, I would strap him into the pushchair and go walking through the city to pass the time. This was the only way I had of finding some calm in my darkest moments.

Once, after a few hours of walking, I decided to catch the bus home. We waited at the stop for a few minutes and I tried to shield the boy from the rain by stretching out the hood of the pushchair. The bus appeared without me noticing, turning the corner faster than usual and stopping in front of us so abruptly that I could hear the passengers inside complaining. For an instant, I imagined an accident in grisly detail: the crash, like an earthquake, my body probably on the ground, head on the road, and from my vantage point, a terrible vision of the little wheels of the pushchair under the bus. I imagined my son's death with horror, and at first, I thought that meant I was a good mother, because I didn't want anything terrible to happen to him, and simply imagining it had caused me inconsolable grief. Then I realised that in my scenario, I was the one who'd been spared. Now, every time I see a mother pushing a pushchair through the city, I wonder what she's thinking about, if she's going somewhere in particular or nowhere at all, if she, too, is trying to escape.

Before I gave birth, I'd imagined life with my son as being similar to treading water in a pool to stay afloat: a constant motion that produces a specific kind of fatigue. It wasn't like that. What had seemed simple—feeding the boy, putting him to bed, keeping him clean, warm, alive—was actually a delicate balancing act. After returning home and receiving visitors, after Miguel's few weeks of paternity leave were up, I was left alone in a barren wasteland of apathy, and everything that should have kept me occupied and alert had an anaesthetic effect on me instead. The days were slow, and they were glum.

The boy showed little interest in latching. After every time I breastfed him and settled him back into the crook of my neck, he would spit up and burst into tears. Before long, the child-themed sheets, his tiny pyjamas, and both of our clothes were covered in stains that didn't come out in the wash. Every day, I placed a plastic bucket, which I had previously used to transport the wet clothes from the washing machine to the drying rack, onto a kitchen scale. I would deposit my son into the bucket wrapped in a thin cotton blanket, hoping for weight gains that never materialised.

In the second month of his life, after a dozen desperate visits to the ER, they discovered that the boy had a minor digestive issue. The knowledge was comforting, or comforting to the mother that I was, it's hard to say why. Maybe it saved me from the feeling that I was losing my mind. They prescribed him hypoallergenic baby formula, which smelled powerfully of synthetic vanilla, and me a psychotropic drug even more stupefying than the one I was already taking to calm my nerves. 'You should have brought him in sooner,' said a nurse. 'The mother should have told us that the child was throwing up like this,' I heard him say to a doctor behind the half-closed door to the office. And 'the mother' turned silent, ashamed, small. Inside her, I followed suit.

Caring for my son entailed a sort of gradual disappearance, and I think I ceased to produce any thoughts other than worries. Whenever someone tried to be understanding or take an interest in how I was doing, specifically whether the boy was letting me get any sleep or whether the care routines were overwhelming, it felt as if they were talking about someone else: the exhaustion in my arms wasn't comparable to the sickly lethargy of my head, something no one ever asked me about.

The boy slept for hours without waking up or bothering me, but our routines were always turbulent in one way or another. Yet, every problem seemed too small to place any real emphasis on, and didn't match up to the effect it was having on me. Things weren't going well because I was inadequate as a mother. I often thought that, one average morning, I would get out of bed and find that the baby had stopped breathing a few hours earlier, that everything would end like that, with me to blame.

One of those mornings, I noticed that the boy's eyelids were coated in a thick green film and rushed him into hospital, leaving the clothes on the floor, the house untidy, the dirty nappies around the bin, and the kitchen window open. They gave him an antibiotic for pink eye and tried to convince me that everything was fine. Moist tear ducts, no fever, good muscle tone, appropriate reflexes. I needn't be alarmed, they told me. I understood then that you can be the inadequate mother who didn't tell them the boy was throwing up like this, at the same time as you can be one of those mothers who will bother the emergency paediatric care department over every little thing. There was no room for ambivalence. Neither of the two mothers received an ounce of compassion, but I think I preferred the reproach of the first time to the condescension of the second.

Nothing I did, nothing I told myself was enough to cast off the feeling that any mistake I made could have horrific consequences. In a moment of disturbing lucidity, I embraced resignation as a strategy. This was no spark of bravery; it was an oversaturation of fear. I accepted my fears and went from being afraid all the time to simply being sad. I decided I would do what I was supposed to: feed the boy when he cried, let him sleep, keep him warm and clean, and hope, day by day, that he didn't stop breathing. I decided not to ask any more questions. I would be a primitive, instinctual mother who didn't think about anything, and I felt that underneath my desperation there might be a glimmer of hope. If that was enough, my son would survive, and if it wasn't, I would wake up one day to find his malnourished corpse in the crib and deal, somehow, with whatever came next.

Night by night, my son never stopped breathing. I guess there were subtle traces of love during that time. They showed themselves in small, occasional ways. Sometimes, when the boy fell asleep at night, I found peace in gazing at him, so calm and content, and I would think that he was perfect and congratulate myself for feeling that way, because it seemed like the way I was supposed to feel. One afternoon, walking through the park with Miguel and the boy, the wind blew off the blanket covering his legs in the pushchair, and I instantaneously tucked it back under his body, then gently touched his face to see if it was cold. The boy looked up at me with his inexpressive, animal eyes and smiled. I saw that it was a genuine smile, directed specifically at me, because he'd recognised me and because he appreciated the pleasant sensations I had just given him. That smile came more and more often as the boy grew, but quickly lost its effect. It became like a stamp: the first time, freshly pressed into the inkpad, his smile was vivid and happy, but every one after that was an increasingly imperfect, muddled copy of that first image, until finally, his smile ceased to mean anything at all.

I've always had a hard time understanding physical affection on an emotional level. Because I generally write in the kitchen, which is in the middle of the house, Carlos will often pass me and lightly stroke my hair, or place a hand on my shoulder. It doesn't bother me, but it only registers in my body and doesn't reach my mind as something that's actually happening. I enunciate every emotion with precise words. Sometimes I ask Carlos, who's more one for intuitive affection and tangible gestures, to tell me in complete sentences what those gestures mean, to tell me that he loves me or misses me. I take more comfort in his explanations. Physical contact is a pleasant bonus, like a soft shirt or the breeze of an air conditioner, but it holds no meaning for me. I could never do this with my son because nothing he did was consistent or structured, and as a result, we couldn't establish any form of communication that was possible for me to translate.

I never recovered my body, and time played its role, too. What had begun as the site of a raging war gradually turned into a familiar landscape that I resigned myself to. The marks of conflict remained in the form of slight changes to the shape of my hips, and in internal scars, which still cause me inopportune pain every so often.

The drive from my home to the private clinic where I'll have an abortion on the first day of winter perfectly matches the length of Supertramp's fourth album. I text Mónica about it as soon as we've parked. She suggests that I could write in some way about what I'm going through. My friends, particularly the ones who don't write, seem to ascribe some curative power to writing. But writing heals nothing; just as it can't cauterise wounds, it can't decisively open them either. Maybe all it does is try to show their particular gleam.

The only form of writing that strikes me as useful are lists. I think of all the births I've been told about at some point, and write in a journal, one after the other, in a vertical line, the names of all the mothers I know: Grandma María, my mother, my aunts, Belinda, a common viper, me. And Celia.

The dot of the 'i' comes out looking like an accent, and I try to correct it with my pen, widening the diameter until it becomes thick and circular, until it covers the initial mark. Then I cross out the entire word and write it again: 'Celia.'

6
CELIA

WHILE THE REST OF US WERE FOURTEEN OR FIFTEEN, CELIA had already turned sixteen and was repeating a year. She came into our lives in September. These two circumstances made her a stranger, but also an authority figure. One spring day on the ramp, she told us she'd met a guy on the internet and that he was her boyfriend now, and my first thought was that I still had yet to get my period, as if the two, getting a boyfriend and getting your period, were linked like a seed and its tree.

Splayed out in the sun before our afternoon classes, time swelled like the asphalt on the main road a couple of hundred metres away from the school patio. Waiting is a place with room for an infinitude of things, because when you're waiting, you feel no urgency to be doing anything else. There was always a tense calm to us during that part of the day, lying against each other, observing each other, sometimes sharing wishes for the future, as if life had yet to happen and we were trying to form a picture of everything to come.

Celia didn't talk about herself much. When she did, she didn't seem to mention the important bits. She'd lived in big cities—at least two—which she talked about casually, as if it was a common experience. I think this was how she talked about everything, and even though I didn't get the impression that she did it so we would admire her sophistication, that was probably the reason why. She pronounced some letters wrong. Her tongue caught against the back of her teeth every time she had to say the "Ce" in her name, and the result, in my ears, sounded very refined. It reminded me a bit of the main characters in Venezuelan telenovelas. Every time I listened to her, I focused on those 'ce's'.

I didn't consider Celia especially pretty, though she was. But I did like her curly blonde hair and the ringlets that fell across her forehead. And her grey eyes, which gave her an intelligent look. Her breasts and hips were shapely in a way that made her look older than me and the rest of the girls. They were as intimidating to me as the transformations taking place in my own body. After the summer holiday, the maths teacher had told me, out of nowhere, that I was one summer away from becoming a woman. It sounded terrifying: an unwanted promise of change. And something else. His words were like the bits of toothpaste that get left behind on your tongue, which you have to swallow without too much thought, despite your disgust.

Sometime before that, my mother had taken me to the gynaecologist for the first time. The gynaecologist was the same doctor who'd brought me into the world, a kind man who I remember nothing else about. He told my mother that at my age I should be wearing bras so that my breasts wouldn't sag as they grew, and my mother bought me some at a store in our neighbourhood. They weren't like the bras Celia wore, with thin straps that you could see on her shoulders. They looked the same as the undershirts I'd always worn, full-length pieces that I put on over my head, the only difference being that they were cut off above the belly button. They were all white and made of cotton, with a shallow sweetheart neckline and an embroidered flower in the middle, or on the elastic trim. I hated them so much that I started hiding them in the back of the wardrobe, along with my childhood blankets.

That afternoon, on our way to the water fountain at the back of the school grounds, just the two of us, Celia told me that the way I dressed hid my true potential. This is how she referred to my body, as something with potential, like a child's body was nothing but what it would become. She asked me if I could keep a secret, which I understood as a sign that she'd taken an interest in me and wanted us to be friends.

While we walked, she criticised my tracksuit bottoms and my shirt and told me what sort of clothes I should be wearing if I wanted to look like her. Bell-bottom jeans elongated your legs and created the illusion of an hourglass silhouette. Platform shoes, covered by the jean bottoms, would give me the extra centimetres I needed to look taller. A cutoff top would show off a bit of my stomach, and a deep neckline—she took my arm as she said this part—would be the finishing touches to a perfect outfit.

I thought about that perfect outfit while I cupped my hands to drink. Celia had drunk before me, straight from the fountain, moving her ponytail out of the way and bringing her lips perilously close to the metallic spout, which one of her hoop earrings clinked against. Once we were done drinking, she took a violet pamphlet that she'd got at the health centre out of her pocket and showed me a tiny white bottle full of round yellow pills. 'They're so you don't get *knocked up*,' she said. I must have looked at her like she was an alien. 'Pregnant, you know?' Two galaxies colliding wouldn't have produced a shock as violent as my world crashing into hers.

There was often a ring of tomato sauce around Celia's mouth. She had this uncanny way of eating spaghetti in the cafeteria; she didn't swirl them with her fork, she got hold of them however she could and brought them to her mouth, slurping from end to end. This is how she got the ring around her mouth. Afterwards, she would wipe off the ring with a napkin, but she never managed to get rid of it entirely. For the rest of the afternoon classes, the ring would still be there on her face. It looked like the remnants of lipstick. That's how I remember her in that moment at the water fountain.

There were all kinds of rumours about Celia. People said, for example, that she was a bit of that word that starts in 's' and ends in 't'—I've always had prudish friends—that she had an older boyfriend, that she went with him in his car to the carpark at the local pool at night, that she wore makeup because she was actually ugly, that her mother or her father—depending on which version—was dead, that they'd found her throwing up in the gym bathroom and that this was an unmistakable sign that she was pregnant. I never found out if any of these rumours were true. The day classes finished, she gave me a small bag with a bit of shiny purple fabric inside it. It was a spandex crop top with a deep neckline, and no label. 'It's a gift, it's for you to wear,' she said, with a wink. I'd never had a crop top before, or anything even close to it. I never heard from her again after that school year. Someone told me she had a son not long afterwards and swore that they'd seen her on the street with a baby in her arms. Some people also said she'd gone to Tenerife to work in a hotel, but I've never been able to confirm either story.

I can't explain why the memory of Celia comes back to me in my darkest moments, like a flower blooming in a strange place, without any relationship between the cause of my darkness and what Celia represents, which is luminous. I don't understand what it is that brings her back to me only on these occasions, and why I forget about her the rest of the time. I've searched for her several times over the past few years, going by her first name and the last name that I remember, though I may not be remembering it right. I want to know more about her, particularly if what people said about her having a child is true or not. If it's true, I calculate that Celia's child would be about fourteen or fifteen now, the same age as I was when I met her. Every so often I ask friends from back then about her, but she doesn't mean anything to them. Sometimes I see a woman who looks like her on the street, or at the dentist, or on the news, in a shot of a busy avenue on the first day of sales, or in a looped set of images of people walking back and forth after an attack in a European city.

Over the weekend in between my first appointment and the date of my surgical abortion, I see my mother and ask her about Celia too. I'm more specific than other times, more insistent, but she doesn't tell me much I haven't already heard. I meet up with her on Saturday at Café Exágono, which isn't called that anymore, in the city's modern district. Celia was pretty—she says—and had grey eyes, peculiar ones—she thinks—and was different from all of us. She feels like she remembers someone telling her that Celia works at a bar in the city named after some place in the U.S., maybe Texas, maybe Alabama, but it's been so long that she might not be remembering right. 'Who knows what happened to her,' she says finally and changes the subject. She asks if I want a ham and cheese sandwich for a snack and she's being serious. When I was nine years old, nothing could have seemed more cosmopolitan to me than spending a Saturday afternoon with my parents in a café with a geometric name, eating a ham and cheese sandwich and drinking a peach juice shaken up for me by a waiter. During the nineties, the names of all the cafés in the area conveyed an unattainable sophistication. Some of them still have that impulse. Some of the people too.

Afterwards, we go Christmas shopping, which is the actual reason for our meeting up. My mother has a shopping list complete with ideas for each member of the family, which suggests I'm in for a long afternoon. She asks my opinion on at least a dozen silk nightgowns for my grandmother María, I suggest CDs and photo books for my sister, scarves for my uncle Pedro, pens with backup ink cartridges for my father, and all sorts of funny, useless knick-knacks for my cousins. Then we spend a little while in a bike shop trying to find the right one for my son, and my mother picks out from the catalogue a cobalt blue bike with a basket on the front and a flashy bell on the handle. They promise they'll have it to us by Christmas Eve.

I go home with her so she doesn't have to carry all the bags herself, and it occurs to me to look through my old bedroom while I wait for my father to get home so I can say hello. Not many of my teenage things are left, because I've got rid of most of them over time, but at the top of the closet, inside a box—I knew it would be there because I've avoided getting rid of it—I find the purple top Celia gave me as a present, now coated in a musty green layer of mildew. I imagine her body in it. I imagine her talking about anything at all and pronouncing her strange, seductive 'ce's.' I imagine her, too, coated in a layer of forgetfulness you can almost feel, like the mildew on the fabric.

7
THE DARKEST MOMENT

MY DARKEST MOMENT CAME ON A SATURDAY NIGHT WHEN THE boy was nine months old. He was playing with a plastic submarine and sitting delicately-balanced in the bath, which was half-filled with hot water. While it continued to fill, I squirted some children's shampoo into the tub to make it a bubble bath. I wanted to surprise him.

The boy welcomed each squirt of shampoo with unintelligible exclamations, and he was awestruck by the waves in the water. There was, in his expression of wonderment, an excitement that I couldn't share. My son's enjoyment left me with a drop of solitude, one that was different to any form of solitude I'd experienced before becoming a mother. Everything felt quietly trivial, and also, somehow, terrible.

The boy was as beautiful as any baby. He wasn't special, though, nor was he as beautiful as he looks in photos. His hair started to fall out in patches not long after he was born and he had a hard time keeping it. There was no hair at all on some parts of his head. The noises he made weren't always pleasant, and his face would scrunch up at the slightest physical effort. There was always something creaturelike about him, an animal quality I found a bit frightening. His moods oscillated between unbridled enthusiasm for an utterly commonplace occurrence, like the shadow of his own feet, and rage at basically any circumstance that bothered him, whatever the reason. There were many times when I thought that there was nothing extraordinary in the transcendental fact of becoming a mother, and that maybe it wasn't my fault. Maybe the boy wasn't capable of awaking in me the same primitive, almost magical emotions that other children awoke in their mothers.

Any minor, accidental scratch inflicted on the boy by the unevenly-filed edges of my nails while I dressed him, or when he robotically brought a toy with sharp corners up to his small mouth, made me feel guilty, as if I was, at every moment, responsible for the preservation of a being that was alive by a miracle, and on top of that, as if he didn't belong to me and I had no right to mess up. All the things my son modified, not just routines, but also, especially, the meanings of trivial things, acted upon me like a thin surface that imprisoned me inside an unpoppable soap bubble, not because it *couldn't* be popped, but because it *shouldn't* be, not in any circumstances, even if the circumstance was that it was what I wanted. When I looked at the boy in the water, damp and shiny, while he sunk his plastic submarine to the bottom of the bathtub only to celebrate its immediate return to the surface, I imagined my fingers as thin as needles, sharp and pointy, that would burst the fragile harmony of our new domestic life, causing it to dissipate with a discrete pop, like a mirage that had never really been there.

The boy's fragility was unquestionable. He was liable to stumble into any sort of accident, any sort of mortal illness, and couldn't defend himself from anything, including me. I plucked him out from the tub and wrapped him in a towel printed with ducks that had a distant look in their eyes. I gave him more physical affection than most days. Then I lathered his body in lotion. I ran a comb through his hair instead of drying it with two brusque shakes of the towel, as I usually did, and then, shiny, dry, and fragrant with children's soap in a clean pair of pyjamas, I handed him over to Miguel like a package. He took over preparing the boy's last bottle of the day and putting him to bed. I put myself to bed, too, covering my head with the duvet and pretending that I was sick and didn't feel like eating dinner. I'm sure I was, because I felt a slight pain in my stomach and other similar symptoms. I turned off the light and lay awake for hours, in silence.

That night, I felt like I couldn't involuntarily open and close my eyes, like I had to work for every blink. It also felt like, if I did close them, I could lose myself in a pitch-black free fall through my own thoughts. There were times back then when I was convinced my body had lost its capacity for any automatic actions, and often, especially at the end of the day, I couldn't get solid foods down without feeling like I was going to choke on every bite, no matter how small. As I lay in bed, I imagined that if I clenched my fists hard enough, I might simply be able to disappear. And I clenched them so hard that I left nail marks in my palms. I also imagined that my heart would stop beating from one moment to the next, or that a blood clot was forming in my brain, and these thoughts brought me something akin to relief, something akin to comfort.

The memories of those months sit in my mind like a collage. I can't describe them in a precise, let alone orderly, way. I don't remember details about my son that other mothers do: whether it hurt when his teeth fell out or not, what kinds of food he liked, if he enjoyed going on walks or hated them. The routines and changes my baby went through in that time, when I think back on them now, are like a cubist painting that combines various settings and objects which don't naturally follow on from one another: a clock sprouting from a tree, an arm that ends in a bell, a uterus containing flowers with long roots floating in the air. Miguel usually took care of all the urgent issues, and I would accompany him in placid silence, entrusting my future to the professional help he had very gingerly suggested I seek out, and that I had accepted.

There are photos of my son from nearly every day of his life. There are at least one or two for every week, detailed documentation of major events like his first day of school or his fifth birthday party, along with the more garden-variety occurrences. My mobile is flooded with his facial expressions and his creations: a structure made of wooden blocks, a doodle of some ships, a smile with a missing tooth. But there's a black hole of photographs between his second or third month of life and his first birthday. The images became less and less frequent from the day he was born onwards;

there were whole months where I didn't take a single picture of him.

I ask Miguel for some photos from back then and he brings me a hard drive with over five-hundred photos of the boy. I barely recognise myself in them. In more recent photos, my son and I often appear holding hands, or spontaneously hugging, or lying on the couch with our heads together. In the photos on Miguel's hard drive, I'm almost always holding the baby by the waist, trying to keep him upright, but also apart from my body. The person behind my smile bears no resemblance to me, yet I wear that same wide, forced grin in every single one of those photos. I wonder why I found it so important to smile for posterity.

I felt like I was playing the role of an impostor, and that feeling arose in many ways. When I took the boy out in the pushchair to go to the grocer's and thanked the older women for their compliments and congratulations on my beautiful boy, I felt it. When I visited the pharmacy to buy those expensive bottles of hypoallergenic baby formula and didn't make a face, I felt it. When I happened to pass by a cinema and was proud not to have cast a single glance at the listing of films I wouldn't have been able to see anyway, I felt it too. I took part in the lie. And the lie was an elephant that lived in the house without anyone willing to point it out, a pink elephant constantly screaming the words: 'There's nothing like motherly love.'

I've never felt motherly love. I've written that sentence many times, in different ways, and have generally accompanied it with a sincere but overwrought plea in my own favour. Sometimes I start to think that you can't produce a sentence like that and leave it by itself, so I add a few extra lines where I mention that things got better, that no one put a name to what was happening to me while it was happening, or offered me help from the beginning, yet still, in spite of it all, I'm not in that place anymore. But when I revise those extra lines, I often delete them. I tend to write them back in a few days later. Whether they'll remain there or not is still an open question for me.

I've never felt motherly love because I don't love my son because I'm his mother, I love him because of who he is; because he doesn't belong to me, he belongs to the world; because I don't instruct him or direct him, I only accompany him, the way he accompanies me. It took me a long time to discover that the bond between the boy and I wasn't necessarily magnetic or magical, much as it may seem that way with other mothers, and in particular, most fictional mothers. That discovery was a revelation: if the bond wasn't hypnotic and instantaneous, then I could, like with anyone else I loved, construct my motherly love for him no differently than someone knitting together fabric to make their first scarf.

When I was little I asked my father to bring me back a doll from one of his trips, and he brought me a wooden train. I guess it must be impossible to instil motherly love with a wooden train, and I started to think that the origins of my insufficiency were rooted in that lack. When the boy was born, I started to think lots of things that I'm ashamed of now. The episode with the doll infuriated me; I wanted a doll so that I could hug it at night and feel like I wasn't sleeping alone. The train was nice, and I pretended it didn't bother me, but whenever I looked at it among all the other toys in my room as a teenager, it reminded me of the solitude of my childhood. I started to refer to that solitude as 'the empty.' Sometimes, when I felt sad, I would cling to my mother's skirt, point to my belly, and say: 'Mamá, the empty is back.' Later, when I was a bit older, they gave me one of those electronic toys with a small screen displaying a pixelated egg or doll that you have to feed and care for. The toy was marketed as a virtual pet and didn't have many functions beyond those two, but depending on the amount of care you provided, the image on the screen would change shape and express certain basic emotions. Every night in bed, I would hold it tight, and I found the most comfort of all in placing it against my heart under my pyjamas and stroking it with my fingers until I fell asleep.

For the first few months after the boy was born, I felt the empty constantly. On the day before the surgical abortion, nearly five years later, the empty is located not in my belly, but in my immediate future. The fact that it's a Sunday aggravates it, especially because it's not an average Sunday, it's the Sunday before Christmas. Most shops stay open on the Sunday before Christmas, and these sorts of exceptions to the norm can be confusing for the unemployed and those of us who make our own work schedules, without a thought for the calendar. I imagine the sensation as being reminiscent of the way a solar eclipse turns the internal clocks of birds haywire, and it's something that has come over me many times before, with similar effects.

In the morning, I take slow steps to the corner shop where I buy bread and fruit every day, trying to take up as much time as possible with each activity so that I won't dwell on tomorrow. On the counter is a carton of cherries from Chile, and I want to buy a few, but the shopkeeper tells me these cherries aren't for me, that I'm best off waiting for the cherries in summer. I tell her that summer fruits are my favourite, and we fall into a conversation about strawberries, raspberries, and varieties of cherries and peaches.

I tell her about the days when I would pick blackberries with my grandmother María behind the fence of their summer house, where the bushes grew intertwined with the metal. She taught me to pick the darkest ones and to forgive the red and the spotted ones, with the hope that they would change colour and turn sweet over the coming weeks. Behind the house was a mountain water spring where my grandmother would wash the blackberries and toss some out; later, we would dust them with sugar.

She once said, I don't know why, that red fruits are food for the magical creatures that inhabit the forest, which annoyed me because I'd always thought magical creatures didn't need food. I mention this to the woman at the corner shop, and she promises to reserve me the first cherries they get in June. I bring home some apples and a slice of orange cake, to nourish my wait.

8
FIRST DAY
OF WINTER

THE BOY WAKES UP EARLY, CONTENTEDLY, ON THE FIRST DAY of winter and asks me how long it is until the school Christmas play and the day he can finally open up the presents under the tree. I tell him there won't be a tree at Grandma María's house—at most there'll be a porcelain Baby Jesus shrouded by a wreath—and that it's only four more sleeps. He's a bit disappointed about the tree, but I try to convince him it will be a festive day: we'll see my parents and my uncles, we'll sing songs, and he'll be able to help my sister prepare the tray of desserts and sweets. The boy asked for a stuffed doll, a picture book with two bears that are friends, and a bike. He repeats his list of presents and counts off on his fingers the nights he has to wait for them.

The instructions for what I have to do before my surgical abortion are precise. I can't eat breakfast or drink liquids. That's easy, because for the past few days I've felt slightly nauseous every time I stand up, a symptom I never had during my pregnancy with my son, nor with the others. I put on comfortable clothes and try to fill every silence with lighthearted chit-chat, I don't want anything I say today to sound serious or deep. I tell Carlos that I'd rather be the one to drive to the clinic which is fine with him, because neither of us particularly loves driving, and I think he's happy not to have to. We drop the boy off at school and I say goodbye the way I always do. 'Have a good day,' I tell him. 'You too,' he replies. This character trait of his never ceases to surprise me: he's excessively courteous, especially in his greetings and farewells. One Sunday morning a few weeks ago, when I dropped him off at Miguel's house, he turned around in the living room as I was leaving, then stood up and said: 'I hope you have a fabulous day.'

I'm dressed too warmly and the car heating makes me feel uncomfortable. Whenever I'm faced with difficult circumstances, I weigh myself down with clothes. Mónica sends a short text message telling me to let her know how it went as soon as I'm out, and I take comfort in the absence of words of encouragement, of any expression of sympathy that might bestow this scene with a pathos that doesn't correspond with it. I can't shake my sense of shame. Because of my error in calculation, because of my intimacy unveiled, because of my carelessness. Never because of guilt or any other sort of moral dilemma.

I'd forgotten how you lose your sense of privacy with procedures like this. With a hospital gown tied round at the back, my body ceases to be mine the moment I cross over the threshold into medical care. I'm afraid that I'll hear the embryo's heartbeat in the preliminary ultrasound and start to think of it as a child, but that doesn't happen; they spare me the excess sentimentality. I choose to be anaesthetised for the operation. Lying on a stretcher, I get a tour of all the ceilings in the facility on my way to the small operating room. The anaesthesiologist asks me to count down from ten to zero, and I watch as he plunges a white sedative into the IV that a nurse had earlier inserted in my arm with a slender needle. I don't feel another thing until I wake up.

I open my eyes feeling a strange agitation in my chest, somewhere that's not the operating room but not a room either. At my side is a doctor that refers to me by too many diminutives, who tells me it's all over and recommends I go home to rest and spend time with my dear ones. I manage to sit up a bit later. I don't notice anything out of the ordinary, except maybe a slight pain in my stomach which intensifies a few hours later, as the painkillers wear off. I get dressed and walk out to the waiting room, to Carlos, who's pretending to read a detective novel. Then he, or I, or both of us, start making stupid jokes that put everything in its right place.

When the boy was born, I never made stupid jokes. Stupid jokes are the lock that closes a darkened room, the threshold I cross to reach the other side. I started to make them one afternoon on the terrace of my flat. The boy and I were lying on a towel taking in the February sun, playing with one of those baby brainteasers with the geometric blocks that you have to slot into a structure with various holes: the star into the star-shaped hole, the triangle into the triangle-shaped hole. The boy was clumsy but persistent and was trying to fit a circular piece into a square hole. At that moment, I saw a repulsive spider crawling determinedly along the edge of the towel, inches away from my son's feet. I'm afraid of spiders—my mother is afraid of them, and so am I, as if I've inherited her primitive fears—but I brought my hand down on it and smashed it against the floor.

The terrifying creature turned into a mess of legs. I cleaned it up with a paper towel that I went inside to retrieve while the boy followed me from one side to another, confidently crawling by then. While I washed my hands, I watched him try to climb up on one of the kitchen cabinets and told him that I could forgive him for the episiotomy I'd had to endure when I gave birth to him, but not for that terrible creature. The boy clapped and smiled, as if he understood, revealing some of the top and bottom teeth that he had grown not long before, and which gave him a friendly look, like a cartoon character. Then he stretched out his arms towards me for me to pick him up, and once he was settled in the crook of my neck, he pointed at the cookie jar on the counter. Months before, his outstretched arms were exactly like spider legs crawling all over me, a threat. That day, they were a source of joy and comfort. I gave him a banana oat cookie, and after he'd sunk his teeth into it and licked it all over, he offered me a bite.

In every journal or other place where I wrote down the things that I would one day want to say about my son, I referred to that specific moment with a brief, but effective note: 'The day with the spider.' I also mentioned it to the psychologist I'd started to see the month before. I wanted to call her and tell her I'd felt like a calm, protective mother for the first time, but I held it in until my appointment. She didn't think much of it. She attributed the improvement to my new medication, which she'd prescribed a few weeks earlier, and said that it was a symptom and not a cause. I don't distrust medication or therapy, but they're invisible, and I have to weave a narrative of concrete symbols around me in order to explain life to myself. I know it was a spider that modified the colour and texture of my days, and that the return of stupid jokes loosened, just a bit, the cord that was tight around my neck.

Sometime later, my son received a little plastic doll's house as a present. Recommended for children nine months and older, it included two medium-sized figures that acted as the parents, a somewhat smaller baby, a cat, and various kitchen appliances and bedroom furniture, which he started to position randomly, coming up with unique combinations: a sink beside a couch, a bed in the middle of the kitchen. The baby was his favourite, and he would constantly move it around the house. One afternoon while I played with him, I tucked the baby into one of the beds and put one of the adult figures into the crib. Highly intrigued, he laughed and became excited, with an animation that reminded me of the expectancy of a dog in front of a chewed-up ball that you're about to throw far into the distance. The boy acted like an adult in the crib was a transgression of the highest order. And more than anything—I'll never forget this—he looked at me with infatuated eyes: I was the funnest person he had ever, and would ever meet, a woman from another world, who could surprise even the best of them with her talent and ingenuity.

Shortly before he turned one, the boy said his first words. Before that, he could blubber out a few stubborn syllables, but he would do it the same way he grabbed whatever small objects were in reach on the table to toss them onto the floor. The syllables were a spoon, a plastic lid, or a clothespin, and the boy had discovered the pleasure of making them his own and tossing them out to see what kind of sound they produced. His first words were conventional (*dada, dog*), no longer loose syllables, and Miguel wrote them all down as they came. Words are important to me, and this register was a staircase made of uneven steps that my son started to climb a little at a time, so that he could relate to me.

The day of his first birthday I took him to see the sea for the first time. I thought it was a nice present. I was sure he wouldn't remember any of it, but I'd be able to tell him about it for years to come, not to mention taking some photos and having him to myself. It was a sunny spring day. Miguel left early for work, and on his way out the door, he reminded me of a few details of the party he'd planned for the afternoon. The boy slept in the car all the way to the beach with his head lolling in his car seat. He wasn't annoyed when I woke him up at my grandparents' summer home. I parked and walked with my son in my arms all the way to the sand. There, we sat on a towel and I took off his shoes. The moment his feet touched the sand he started sobbing inconsolably, genuinely panicked by the strange, unfamiliar material all around us, and he climbed up around my neck again. I took him to the edge of the water and he wanted to get down immediately. He didn't fuss about the temperature or the waves, celebrating them with gusto, and he liked the wet sand, which was dense and more reliable. Holding me by the hand, he took a few tentative steps and said 'water,' and said 'yes,' and said 'mummy, water,' and said 'come,' and said 'mummy come,' motioning for us to go further in. That was when I knew, for the first time, that I had someplace to go.

For the first few hours after the surgical abortion, I lie in bed, rain pattering against the window. Miguel picks the boy up from school like any other Monday, and I receive a voice message where they both sing me a horrible Christmas song about a lamb and a bell. I fall asleep after that, in the silence of the childless home. As night falls, I pick up a sock he left on the couch, along with a rubber horse that had been abandoned on the floor, a book about elephants which was open on the rug, and a convertible toy car left in front of his bedroom door. The childless home would be a good place for an archeologist: the traces of his activity linger even when he's not around. These objects, along with his clothes, particularly his tiny shoes, provide a window into his habits.

The boy and I don't always look like other children and other mothers, if there really are children and mothers who resemble each other. We're equal beings who don't seek to impose our will on one another, even though I'm the one who decides when it's time to go to bed and who picks what foods he can and can't eat. I bring him with me to bookshops and he entertains himself while I read the first page of a novel. I teach him only the songs I like, and we don't spend much time in playgrounds. Instead, I buy cups and plates decorated with elephants and planes and find myself hard-pressed to find a single piece of normal kitchenware when-ever I invite an adult over for lunch. And when he asks me if I've ever dreamt of having a flying bicycle, I don't respond mindlessly, I take my time to think and tell him that it seems like an uncomfortable system and that if I wanted to fly through the city I'd rather have a hot air balloon. We build our world together, like an intermediary zone between what he needs and wants and what I want and need. Mothers are supposed to build a nest out of bits of wood and cardboard to care for their eggs and offspring. My son and I built that nest together, to meet our needs and care for one another.

On the night of the first day of winter, my mother calls me in good spirits to tell me she bought a small plastic Christmas tree, and that the boy will be able to open his presents under it, which is a wish he has repeated constantly for the past few weeks. The bicycle she picked out for him is bigger than the tree, but I don't mention it. What for?

9
A BOAT

I SLEEP FITFULLY, MY DREAMS AGITATED. ON THE TWENTY-second of December, when I wake up, I discover a patch of blood on the flannel sheets and rip them off the bed in embarrassment, like I've just gotten my first period. Carlos went to work a few hours ago, before dawn. My stomach is inflamed, and although the pain is manageable and the clinic told me I might experience some bleeding, I call Mónica to ask if it's all normal, and then write to my yoga teacher to tell her not to expect me until after Christmas.

Later, the postman delivers a medium-sized package to the door. I like him, he's friendly. He tends to be cautious when he slides the post through our postbox downstairs, and if it doesn't fit, he doesn't force the packages by the corners: instead, he comes up to hand them to me in person. Usually, he stops for a bit of small talk, and always says goodbye with a 'so long' and a slight wave.

The postman talks to me briefly about the fog. I tell him that I saw a crane towering over the roofs of the lower city through my window a few hours ago. The fog covered it all, from the feet of the buildings in my neighbourhood, up to the mountain and beyond. In the middle of that expanse, the crane's two cables suspended a blue metal waste collector with construction materials inside it. The cables attached to either side of the collector and the top of the crane formed the outline of a triangle like the sail of a sailboat. The waste collector was the hull, and it floated on the fog like it was navigating the river that separates the world of the living—the world of chimneys and the satellite dishes beside them—from the world of the dead—the world of the shopping centre lights in the distance. Some birds were perched on top of it. I show the postman a photo on my phone: 'A boat,' I say. He asks where. 'It's in the way you look at it,' I reply. And then he says, 'So long, boat,' and walks off with a wave of his hand, like always.

One of the first things we teach babies are the words and gestures for greetings and farewells, which are practically universal. They learn *hello* and *goodbye* at almost the same time as they do *yes* and *no*. It's important to know how to leave, how to say goodbye. Phone conversations, for example, don't end until one of the two people on the line works up the courage to say the words after an uncomfortable, inconclusive silence, and the other person tends to receive them with relief. These parts of conversations are typically omitted in fiction, but they're the parts that interest me most. Goodbye rituals are precise and always recur in the same way, whether the farewell is definitive or temporary.

The package contains four copies of a slender book of poems I translated into Galician and a tulip bulb wrapped in a yellow draw-string bag. Isabel, the editor, told me she was sending the books, but hadn't mentioned the tulip bulb, so it was a surprise. It was also a commitment—a seed always is.

When my grandmother María built her house, she wanted to plant a garden with nothing but trees and flowering bushes, and no vegetable patch. She didn't want to have to harvest anything useful from the soil. But beauty was extremely important to her, or that's my impression. There have always been flowerpots in her house, and little sacks of seeds for all kinds of flowers in the kitchen cabinets, and she plants these seeds every so often, when the season comes around. Someone once gave her an orange tree that never produced fruit for the garden, and I think that made her happy.

A few years ago she told me that when she was a girl, her school teacher had handed out branded pencils from the local liquor factory to the students. She described them to me in detail. They were a bit shorter than your average pencil and made of a light-coloured wood; on the side was the name of the factory, and near the end, an elderflower in black, with a bird of the same colour perched atop it. The teacher had handed out the pencils for them to do their schoolwork with, but she saw how fascinated my grandmother was by hers, and how afraid she was of writing with it, of losing it forever after too many sharpenings. Without any of the other children noticing, the teacher gave her a second pencil and said: 'One for you to write with, the other for you to keep.' This was a revelation for my grandmother María: 'Finally, I had something beautiful of my own.' I think beauty should be an unquestionable right, something we can all pursue and keep.

I stored the tulip bulb Isabel had sent me in my nightstand, and thought for a moment about the importance of summoning up the tenderness it deserved to be planted with.

While I was doing all these things, my uncle Pedro was taking my grandmother María to the hospital for a high fever. He told me at midday. It was nothing serious, a common infection, yet her organs started to fail one after another over the course of the day, and she wasn't responding to the antibiotics. My father went to visit her a few hours later, when the end seemed near, though it still wasn't inconceivable that she might recover. Once she lost consciousness, they admitted her to the intensive care unit and no one was allowed to be with her outside of visiting hours. My father told me that she seemed calm, sleepy, and that she opened her eyes occasionally but it was hard to say if she could tell you were there.

I've always had an aversion, when death seems near, to the anticipation of grief. When my father tells me that my grandmother is calm and sleepy, that it had to happen eventually, that I should know it's possible she won't wake up again, my thoughts immediately turn to how I'll arrange my domestic life to attend the wake for a death that has yet to occur. I think about how best to tell my son, assuming it happens, and feel ashamed for my mind turning to these thoughts. I pick the boy up from school, take him to see a film about talking planes, and then back home, I feed him dinner and put him to bed without telling him a story. I also clean the glass in the shower and the bathroom mirror, leaving them spotless, without a water droplet in sight.

There's a certain kind of sadness associated with fever. A shivering sadness. The spasms and the fear brought on by that sadness are neither controllable nor predictable. A pot takes the same amount of time to boil whether you're watching it or not, but an imminent death could convince you otherwise. In the early hours of the morning on the twenty-third, my grandmother dies while I'm asleep. I, too, have a fever that night, a few tenths of a degree too high.

There's an abruptness to feverish sadness. It's how my body prepares me for nostalgia, how it talks to me, how it says: *you should know* something is happening. When I find out, early in the morning, my house is in complete silence and my son is still asleep. It's the last day of school before the winter holidays. I make myself coffee and sit on the living room sofa waiting for him to wake up. While I wait, I search voraciously among the books on my shelves for two very specific poems. They're certainly not the best poems about grief, not even the best that I can personally think of, but they give me comfort in those first few hours.

I try to remember a prayer, but none come to mind. My grandmother knew lots of them, and whenever she uttered one of the prayers dedicated to the Virgin Mary, mother of mothers, I thought that she was singing it to herself, she too being the mother of mothers, the first mother in my line, or something like that. Then I remember the tulip bulb that came in Isabel's package. I tuck it into the soil in a planter on the kitchen windowsill, so that it can await the spring. I touch my forehead with my hands and it's burning up. The motion leaves a dark streak of wet soil on my forehead, and after that, nothing extraordinary happens.

I'm struck again by the sounds of death at my grandmother's wake, the silence broken by the discrete footsteps of the funeral home employees, the moment when the condolences turn into trivial conversations.

I go by myself, well dressed in a dark grey jacket and with my hair in a high ponytail. When someone dies, I always remember two details: how I dressed and how I wore my hair. They're coordinates I can use to locate my state of mind during that time. My grandmother said that you have to wear discreet colours to funerals, but never pure black, because black shows an excessive form of grief, one that's gone out of fashion.

I explain it to the boy in simple terms. I tell him that Grandma María isn't here anymore, that her body stopped working and that now we can remember what she was like, but we can't visit her. The boy doesn't understand death, and he fears it, because he's better acquainted with it than he should be. He asks every so often about my aunt and about my grandfather or his—Miguel's father, who died when he was a few months old. He has a theory that births and deaths are like mutually agreed-upon entries and exits from a boat with limited space. When someone dies, another person has to be born to take their place, but likewise, when someone is born, someone has to die to make room for them. He asks where Grandma María is and I promise to take him to the cemetery one day, hoping that he'll forget all about it.

The festivities of the next few days are partly suspended. We bury my grandmother the afternoon of Christmas Eve, at a cemetery that's emptier than usual. On Christmas Day, my uncle Pedro grills meat and makes a salad for everyone, and with my son's help, my sister prepares the tray of desserts, despite the circumstances. We all eat lunch together, respecting my grandmother María's empty seat and being there for one another. We open presents, and my son is delighted to find the stuffed doll, the book with the bears, and the blue bicycle, sitting beside the baby Jesus shrouded by a yellow wreath. No one remembers the plastic tree my mother bought. Not even the boy.

Over the next few days of December, before Lucía's wedding and my trip to Madrid, it snows in lots of places, but not here. It snows in the mountains and in cities my son has never been to. We see pictures in the paper and on the news. The boy asks if the snow is made on a computer, like everything he sees on TV. He yearned so deeply for snow over those days that I started to think it would snow for us, too, and that longing was as important a factor as the temperature.

In the window of his room, I let him hang a drawing he made with coloured pencils. It's a crimson bird with fantastical feathers and a crown around its head. I write beside the bird: 'Hello, snow,' inviting it to fall. As if writing could turn the rain into something else. As if writing could bring something to life where there had formerly been nothing but a seed or an expectation. As if writing were a promise.

There's a joyful tone to the news reports about the snow, photos of snowmen being made by children in parks and footage of collective games played in city streets. Still, I'm not sure that falling snow is a happy occurrence. I think of the fallen trees, of the grit that it becomes mixed with. But also the whiteness, the strangeness, the landscape.

On one of these nights, the boy says he wants to talk about Grandma María all the time so that we don't forget what she was like. He asks me if it makes me sad for us to talk about Grandma María all the time so that we don't forget what she was like. As with the snow, I 'm not sure whether this is a sad, or a happy thing.

What isn't happy, by any means, is a nostalgia that cannot be appeased.

10
CONFETTI

ON THE TWENTY-NINTH OF DECEMBER, A FEW HOURS BEFORE boarding my train to Madrid for Lucía's wedding the next day, I stroll through an empty park with Miguel and the boy. The boy wants to try out his new bike, and Miguel asks that he not to go too far, that he pedals in circles around us while we sit on a bench. Hands stiff from the cold, I say goodbye to them at Miguel's house and agree to pick up my son the morning of New Year's Day. I promise the boy that we'll take our bikes out to the park together and that we can go wherever he likes, riding one after the other, because bikes aren't fun if they aren't taking you somewhere.

I'm on the verge of telling Miguel everything that's happened over the past few days, of telling him about my visit to the clinic, about the abortion, about the strange nostalgia that settled into my chest once the blood and stomach pains had eased to the point of fading completely. In a certain sense, we're still travel companions, because we accompany the same boy on his path through life. And in a certain sense, we love each other more than we used to, after we worked up the courage to say we didn't love each other anymore, and that's why I want to tell him about it, though I decide not to in the end. I guess silence is another thing we share, and that's okay (in a certain sense).

The empty has taken on a strange shape now. What had started as a conflict, a scary expectation, made more vivid by the memory of my first months with my son and the certainty that I'm not a good enough mother for a baby, has morphed into something else, an ambiguous grief. I begin to think that it's still sad even though I don't want another child, the absence of something that could have been and isn't, its discrete disappearance. Now that the problem has gone, in comes the fantasy, the hypothesis, the opportunity for a different story, one that no longer scares me because it's an impossibility. I imagine Carlos caring for a little girl with curious eyes, the two of us taking her to see fireworks for the first time, or the boy playing with a smaller boy who looks a bit like him.

I imagine my family as a row of dominoes, with my son as the last one. The death of my grandmother María has brought an end to everything that came before me, because my past stretches only as far back as my parents can remember. My grandmother was the first domino, and my parents will be the next to fall, sometime in a too-near future. I'm in the middle of the row, between my son and my parents. Maybe, I find myself thinking, I was supposed to add more dominoes, to extend the legacy of my fallen loved ones a bit further.

Late in the morning, a deliveryman in uniform comes to the door holding a large, rectangular package with my name on it. I'm not sure what it is, but after I cut open the tape on the cardboard box, I find a piece of silk paper wrapped around a doll: the silicone baby I'd ordered one night last week, as a Christmas present for my grandmother. I'd completely forgotten about it and I don't know what to do with it at first. Without stopping to look at it for too long, I decide to pack it into the suitcase I'm bringing with me on my trip, which is practically empty. The doll is dressed in a white onesie with yellow stripes. Inside the box is a card that reads, in ugly, bulging letters: 'Adoption Certificate,' and a baby sling. It reminds me of my son, of all the things I didn't do with him, but also of all the things I'll never do with the second child that no longer exists.

I catch the train at three in the afternoon on a Tuesday, surrounded by happy people. The heat and vapour swirling around the train carriage induce a gentle, pleasant lightheadedness in me, a fog that feels like it's emanating from my head or my body rather than from my surroundings. During the train journey, I imagine walking through Madrid with the doll around my neck, or wrapped in a cotton blanket, or in the baby sling I brought with me. It doesn't particularly bother me that the idea might be disturbing, although it does scare me to think that in a moment of carelessness, someone on the street might notice the baby isn't real and say something to me about it. Or that they won't say a word to me and will simply mutter to themselves about it as they walk by.

The hotel room, on the southern outskirts of the city, has only one window, which looks out onto an interior patio. I call Lucía to let her know I've arrived and tell her how excited I am to celebrate her wedding and that I'll see her in a matter of hours. Then I take the doll out of my suitcase and examine it slowly. I suppose they meant for it to be a girl: there are silver earrings in its ears in the shape of tiny flowers, which I would never put on my daughter, if I had one.

I lie in the hotel bed thinking about how I won't be able to sleep bundled up in the blankets and my thermal pyjamas, with their synthetic fabric, which I packed because I assumed it would be cold in the city. The fabric doesn't feel good on my skin and as always when an unpleasant sensation coincides with my sleep time, I have an unsettling nightmare. I dream that my son and I are on a train, or not exactly my son, but some other boy maybe a year or two younger than him. At first the boy walks, then runs through the train carriage, and I chastise him, pick him up, and caress him. He sits up on his knees and leans his head against the window to look outside, his breath fogging up the glass. Then I rock him until he falls asleep. Once he has, and is still glued to me, the boy's skin starts to turn cold and there's nothing I can do to stop it. I try to warm him up, first with my body and then by wrapping him in a blanket. My boy is cold and I need to warm him up. Finally, I wake up drenched in sweat, my breathing heavy. I rip off the pyjamas and get into the shower.

Maybe because my mind is infested with sensations from the dream, or maybe because it's still very early and I assume there won't be many people out, I don't question my impulse to take the doll out in the baby sling and go for a walk through the park by the hotel, a pedestrian area that spans either side of the Manzanares River. Using the hair dryer in the bathroom,

I apply heat to its silicone skin. I put on my coat and walk to a secluded spot. There, I find a woman running around in circles, but no passersby who'll pay any attention to me. At first, the feeling is pleasant. The sensation reminds me of carrying a living child, particularly the heat, which quickly dissipates, and the weight, which is that of a few-months-old baby.

What had begun as placid, despite my agitation, gradually shifts into an oppressive discomfort. Grief washes over me like it has at other times, without warning, in the form of an incapacity to simply do what it takes to stay alive: breathe, move my arms and legs in sync with the rest of my body, make simple decisions, blink automatically. Sitting on a bench by the river, I remove the doll from the carrier. I take its clothes off to look inside it and discover that its body is a sack of fabric, most likely full of sand. I wonder if it would be easier like this, for us to be born with a lump of fabric for a heart. A few hours after my grandmother was admitted to the hospital, my uncle Pedro told me that the doctors had noticed in one of the tests that her heart was larger than normal. The human heart swells when it suffers. Mónica explained that to me, and I didn't understand what possible advantages it could have.

No one sees, I don't think, when I hurl the doll into the bottom of the river.

When I was little, my grandmother told me a story that began like this: 'There's a river that makes you lose your memory of the other side if you cross it.' I can't continue the story, I guess because I never wanted to cross that river.

In the darkness of the hotel room, I hug my legs and spend the morning in that position, hardly moving, thinking occasionally about the doll at the bottom of the river and the ashes of my aunt and grandfather standing in urns beside my grandmother María's coffin. Eyes closed, I imagine that I too am at the bottom of a river, that I've achieved absolute stillness. I imagine myself as ash, and that the darkness where I am is the same as the darkness of my fictitious child, that we share the depths of a forest we should never have entered. I'm not going to go to Lucía's wedding. I text her with an excuse about coming down with severe food poisoning.

I review, in silence, the list of my dear ones, the list of my living and my broken bonds. It's important to have a final resting place, and the difference between the dead and the disappeared is, precisely, the place that the disappeared don't occupy. Children that never came to be have no place. Nor does Celia, nor her living or fictitious child, though the memory of her barges back into my mind and occupies it completely, like an overly large piece of furniture in a bedroom.

I'm returning home on the last day of the year, and there's a man buying some presents in the train station shop at midday. He labours over his selections of a stuffed elephant, a toy car, a rubber bath toy, things like that, and then asks for them all to be gift-wrapped. Every time I travel, I assume that the other passengers I encounter are on a similar journey, that they leave when I leave and return when I return, independent of where they're coming from or going to. I assume the man in the shop is buying presents for his children, though I'm not sure if they're Christmas presents or souvenirs from his trip. I assume he's a good man, but maybe he's like me: one of those inconsiderate people who'll buy whatever they can find at the last minute and show up at a family celebration with ugly toys far too childish for their now-teenage nieces and nephews. I'll never know.

I catch the return train at three in the afternoon. My seat is facing the opposite direction of the train's movement, which doesn't bother me, though at another point in time I would have begged someone to swap places There's a festive atmosphere in the carriages, groups of animated people, as well as solitary individuals longing for the trip to pass quickly so they can reunite with whoever is surely waiting for them at their destination. It's easy to see by their expressions what the promise of a few days spent with family does for these people. I fall asleep with my headphones in and a novel covering my face.

In the middle of the journey, late into the afternoon, the train stops due to the snow. I'm woken by the rest of the passengers as they loudly inform people on their phones what's happened, furious with the train company over a meteorological event. The landscape outside the window is beautiful, slightly white amidst the darkness starting to fall over the fields, impossible to tell which falls first, the night or the snow. The waiting soothes me, and my eyes fall upon an older woman who has remained silent, not complaining about anything. After a little over an hour the train gets moving again.

It's nearly midnight by the time we reach the city. I walk down the dark, silent, deserted streets. I'm in no rush to get home. Maybe it's sad to arrive at a train station where no one is waiting for you. But I travel alone a lot, and I've learned not to confuse sadness with disappointment or the desire for something else. Cold as it is, the night is also gently beautiful. I look out at buildings I've seen many times before as if they're a sketch or a film set. I have an urge to message Carlos, who's at dinner with his family, but I'd rather he imagine me tired and laughing in the well-worn formal dress from my suitcase, and not glum and lonely on my way back to our flat. The lights of the bars on the outskirts, some of them about to open, take me by surprise, and I hear voices and applause at the back of a dead-end alley, most likely from a celebration in a bar I can't see but can guess is there. I walk in the direction of the sound and discover, on the slightly illuminated sign, a drawing of a mountain and blue words that allude to some place in North America; I can't remember where, maybe Texas, maybe Alabama, but I think it was Nebraska. Inside, a group of men are watching the twelve chimes of the bell signalling the final night of the year. They all have paper party hats on their heads and shaky smiles on their faces. These are people destined to spend special days in any sad, poorly-lit dive bar in the world, without the company of their dear ones. Like me.

A blonde waitress with curly hair and grey eyes, wearing a cutoff top with a beaded neckline and a pair of jeans, stares at the TV out of the corner of her eye. She's holding a metal tray between her arm and her body, and is holding a plastic bag with tinsel and other shiny things in it. I ask her name, expecting to hear her drawled 'ce's' and for her electric eyes to fall on me, to recognise me. She responds in an Italian accent with enormous vowels that throws me off balance, says her name is Bianca and asks do I want anything to drink. Her eyes aren't grey, they're blue, and her hair doesn't look as blonde in the fluorescent lighting overhead. Festive music blares from the television. The men clink their glasses in a clumsy toast, and the unfamiliar waitress shakes the plastic bag in the air, creating a cloud of tinsel.

And, around my head, falls a delicate ring of confetti.

THE TULIP I PLANTED IN DECEMBER IN A POT ON THE KITCHEN windowsill, or rather, the flower of that tulip bulb, bloomed in early March. Its stalk was short, and I cut it as soon as the petals began to unfurl. I placed it in a tall vase on top of my nightstand.

Whenever I put flowers in water, I always leave a split aspirin tablet at the bottom of the vase. My grandmother told me this was a way to keep them alive for a few days longer. I find the act of putting flowers in water moving, but what's even more moving to me is the aspirin. It makes me sad to see the way the tulips look outside the soil, rootless, without anything linking them to the earth, until they wilt completely. It's heartbreaking that we cut a flower's bonds so that it'll be beautiful by our side.

I finished writing this book on the second of May, the first Sunday of the month. For Mother's Day, my son gave me a drawing he'd made at school. In it are he and I and a vertical line running down the middle of the page from top to bottom. On the other side of the line are Miguel and Carlos.

He drew a circle that looks like a ball in the air, and over my head, a clumsy pink heart. He pointed at the middle of the drawing and said: 'We're playing volleyball.' Then he added: 'This is our net.' And I said yes, yes it was, that was our net.

Postpartum depression is the number one cause of death in mothers during the perinatal period in most Western countries, above hypertension and haemorrhaging.

I wrote this book because I'm alive.

BERTA DÁVILA (SANTIAGO DE COMPOSTELA, 1987) IS A WRITER and poet. With *O Derradeiro Libro de Emma Olsen* (2013) she won the prize of the Galician Publishers' Association for the best book of fiction. For *Carrusel* (2019) she received the Manuel García Barros Novel Prize and the Premio de la Crítica española de narrativa en lengua gallega, which she also won in the poetry category for her collection *Raíz da Fenda* (2013). Her novel *Illa Decepción* (2020) won the Repsol Short Story Prize. *Os Seres Queridos*, winner of the Xerais Novel Prize, is her latest book.

JACOB ROGERS IS A TRANSLATOR OF GALICIAN AND SPANISH literature. He has been awarded grants by the National Endowment for the Arts and the PEN/Heim Translation fund. He has also co-edited features of Galician literature for Words Without Borders, Asymptote, and The Riveter.

We translate female authors who write in minority languages. Only women. Only minority languages. This is our choice.

We know that we only win if we all win, that's why we are proud to be fair trade publishers. And we are committed to supporting organisations in the UK that help women to live freely and with dignity.

We are 3TimesRebel.